Geilles Herring

An Irish Cousin

Vol. I.

Geilles Herring

An Irish Cousin
Vol. I.

ISBN/EAN: 9783337125844

Printed in Europe, USA, Canada, Australia, Japan

Cover: Foto ©Andreas Hilbeck / pixelio.de

More available books at **www.hansebooks.com**

BY

GEILLES HERRING AND MARTIN ROSS.

IN TWO VOLUMES.

VOL. I.

LONDON:

RICHARD BENTLEY AND SON,

Publishers in Ordinary to Her Majesty the Queen.

1889.

CONTENTS.

PART I.

AN EXPERIMENT.

CHAPTER I.

"In that new world which was the old."

CHAPTER II.

"Sing Hey! when I preside."

CHAPTER III.

"Willy's fair and Willy's rare,
And Willy's wondrous bonny."

CHAPTER IV.

"My father's brother; but no more like my father than I
to Hercules."

CHAPTER V.

" Groping in the windy stair,
Darkness and the breath of space
Like loud waters everywhere."

CHAPTER VI.

" In Islington there was a man,
Of whom the world might say,
That still a godly race he ran,
Whene'er he went to pray."

CHAPTER VII.

" Or in the night, imagining some fear,
How easy is a bush suppos'd a bear! "

CHAPTER VIII.

" Rode he on Barbary? Tell me, gentle friend,
How went he under him ? "

" This is the prettiest low-born lass——"

CHAPTER IX.

"*Ford.* Old woman! What old woman's that?

. . . .

A witch, a quean, an old cozening quean!
Have I not forbid her my house?"

CHAPTER X.

"On the first day of spring, in the year '93,
The first recreation in this countheree,
The King's counthry gintlemen o'er hills, dales, and rocks,
They rode out so gallant in search of a fox."

CHAPTER XI.

"He is the toniest aristocrat on the boat."

CHAPTER XII.

"And wouldst thou leave me thus? Say Nay."

CHAPTER XIII.

"Go, let him have a table by himself!
For he does neither affect company,
Nor is he fit for't, indeed."

CONTENTS.

CHAPTER XIV.

"Ah! Then was it all spring weather?
Nay, but we were young and together."

"Society is now one polished horde
Formed of two mighty tribes, the Bores and Bored."

CHAPTER XV.

"She's always been kind of off-ish and partic'lar for a gal
that's raised in the woods."

CHAPTER XVI.

"I do perceive here a divided duty."

CHAPTER XVII.

"The tenacious depths of the quicksand, as is usual in such
cases, retained their prey."

PART II.

THE COST OF IT.

CHAPTER I.

"Fate's a fiddler, life's a dance."

"O'Rorke's noble feast will ne'er be forgot
By those who were there, and those who were not."

AN IRISH COUSIN.

PART I.

AN EXPERIMENT.

CHAPTER I.

THE "ALASKA."

"In that new world which was the old."

THERE had been several days of thick, murky weather—dull, uncomplaining days that bore their burden of fog and rain in monotonous endurance. Six of such I had lived through; a passive existence, parcelled out to me by the uncomprehended clanging of bells, and the, to me, still more incomprehensible clatter which, recurring at regular intervals, told that a hungry multitude were plying their knives and forks in the saloon.

But a change had come at last; and on Saturday morning, instead of the usual heaving ridges of grey water, I saw through the port-hole the broken green glitter of sunlit waves. The s.s. *Alaska's* lurching plunge had subsided into a smooth unimpeded rushing through the water, and for the first time since I had left New York, the desire for food and human companionship awoke in me.

" Stewardess," I said, " get me a cup of tea.   I am going on deck."

It was early when I came on deck. The sun was still low in the south-east, and was spreading a long road of rays toward us, up which the big steamer was hurrying, dividing the radiancy into shining lines, that writhed backwards from her bows till they were lost in the foaming turmoil astern.

A light north wind was blowing from a low-lying coast on our left, bringing, as I fancied, some faint suggestion of fields and woods. I walked across the snowy deck, to where a sailor was engaged in a sailor's seemingly invariable occupation of coiling a rope in a neat circle.

" I suppose that is Ireland ? " I said, pointing to the land.

" Yes, miss ; that's the county Cork right enough. We'll be into Queenstown in a matter of three hours now."

" Three hours more ! " I said to myself. while I watched the headlands slowly changing their shapes as we steamed past. It would soon begin now, this new phase of my life, whether I wished it or not. It had once seemed impossible ; now it was inevitable. My destiny was no longer in my own control, and its secret was, perhaps. hidden among those blue Irish hills, which looked as if they were waiting for me to come and prove what they had in store for me.

"Well, it has been my own doing," I thought; "whatever comes of it, I have only myself to thank; and whether they like or dislike me, I shall have to make the best of them, and they of me."

"First breakfast just ready, miss," said one of the innumerable ship-stewards, scurrying past me with cups of tea on a tray.

I paid no attention to the suggestion, and made my way to a deck chair just vacated by an elderly gentleman. I could not bring myself to go below. The fresh sweet wind, the seagulls glancing against the blue sky, the sunshine that gleamed broadly from the water and made a dazzling mimic sun of each knob and point of brasswork about the ship,—to exchange these for the fumes of bacon and eggs, and the undesired conversation of some chance fellow-passenger, seemed out of the question.

Moreover, I was too restless and excited to care about breakfast just then. The sight of the land had given new life to expectations and hopes from which most of the glory had departed during the ignominious misery of the last six days. I lay in my deck chair, idly watching the black river of smoke that streamed back from the funnels, and for the first time found a certain dubious enjoyment in the motion of the vessel, as she progressed with that slight roll in her gait which the sea confers upon all its *habitués*.

Most people appear to think that sea-sickness, if spoken of at all, should be treated as an involuntarily comic episode, to be dealt with in a facetious manner.

But for me it has only two aspects—the pathetic and the revolting; the former being the point of view from which I regard my own sufferings, and the latter having reference to those of others. In the dark hours spent in my state-room, I had had abundant opportunity to formulate and verify this theory, and I have never since then seen any reason to depart from it.

CHAPTER II.

AUNT JANE.

"Sing Hey! when I preside."

IT may not be a very dignified admission, but one of the main causes that led to my being at present on board the *Alaska*, bound for Queenstown, was the incompatibility of my temper with that of my Aunt Jane.

In self-extenuation, I may mention that I had for the last twelve months lived in her house, and had thus had ample opportunity of verifying the opinion expressed by many of her most intimate friends—"That Jane Farquharson was the salt of the earth, but as such was better when taken in very small quantities."

She was a Scotchwoman of the most inflexible type. Twenty-five years of sojourn in the United States had modified none of her insular prejudices, and my mother, who was her youngest sister, had never, even during her married life, lost belief in the awfulness of her authority.

The Farquharsons were a family whose pedigree was longer than their purse ; and when her younger brother, my Uncle James, had been compelled to sell the paternal acres and emigrate to California, my aunt had uprooted herself from her native land and followed his fortunes, in the full conviction that he, excellent young man though he was, would become altogether a castaway if once allowed out of range of her vigilant eye. They were orphans, and Aunt Jane, having imposed upon herself the duties of both parents, took my mother with her to the Far West, where she maintained on my uncle's ranch the straitest traditions of the elders.

Uncle James never married. Aunt Jane's vigilance had been so conscientiously unremitting that no daughter of Heth had ever disputed with her the position of mistress of Farquharson's ranch. But the precautionary measures that had preserved Uncle James from the snares of matrimony were a distinct failure in my mother's case. With the unexpected revolt of a weak nature, she defied her elder sister, and committed the incredible enormity of getting married.

Men—with the exception of a legendary Scotch minister, who, if tradition spoke truly, had not long survived his betrothal to Aunt Jane—were regarded by her as the natural foes of cleanliness, economy, and piety. And of all men she considered Irishmen to be the epitome of their sex's atrocities.

It must, then, be admitted that Fate dealt hardly with Aunt Jane, when, one summer afternoon, her sister Helen came to her and told her that she had that morning been married to Owen Sarsfield, the good-looking Irishman who, a few months before, had entered into partnership with their brother. My mother has often described the scene to me—how she had found Aunt Jane grimly darning her brother's socks; how she had received the news at first in terrible silence; and then how on my mother, white and trembling, had fallen the thunders of her wrath.

"That ne'er-do-weel Irishman! A creature that 'tis well known had to leave his home for Heaven only knows what wickedness! Did you never hear that a bad son makes a bad husband? I was right when I warned James against having anything to do with a vagabond scamp such as he is, and told him no good would come of handling money that had doubtless been won at the gaming-table!"

To all this, and much more, my mother did not attempt a reply; she thought she knew more of Owen Sarsfield than her sister did. She and her husband settled down in another house on the ranch, and, notwithstanding their proximity to Aunt Jane, they were very happy.

My father, in spite of Aunt Jane's insinuations to the contrary, was an Irish gentleman of good family, and the money which he had put into the farm had been honestly come by. Perhaps my mother never knew the exact reason of his leaving Ireland. She only told me that money troubles had led to a quarrel with his father, Theodore Sarsfield, of Durrus, in the county Cork. He had no sisters, and his younger and only brother, Dominick, had sided with my grandfather against him, so that during the fifteen years he had spent in America he was as much cut off from his home as if he had been on another planet. The little that he knew of it was gathered from a few misspelt letters, written by one Patrick Roche, a special retainer of his in the old days at Durrus.

These reached him at long intervals, and usually announced some event connected with the Sarsfield family. In this way he heard of his brother's marriage, which took place three or four years before his own. Then shortly afterwards, towards the end of the Irish famine, came the news that "The young misthris was ded, and she just after havin' a fine young son; 'twas what the peepel war all saying that the hard times kilt her."

My mother used sometimes to take these letters from a little old green velvet bag in which she hoarded many valueless treasures, and give them to me to read. And I well remember the yellow worn papers, with the half-foreign smell of turf-smoke lingering about them. I did not then dream of how, in after-years, when that same smell of turf-smoke became very familiar, it would recall the hours I spent when a child, sitting in the shade of the verandah beside my mother's rocking-chair, and poring with subdued excitement over these messages from the other side of the world.

The last letter which my father received was as urgent as it was brief.

"HONORED MASTHER OWEN" (it began, without any of the usual preamble of good wishes),

"The owld masther is very sick. You'd do well to cum home. Ther is them that sayes he's askin' for you, and

God knows maybe 'tis the change for deth that's on him. The family is very poor this while back. The big house do be mostly shut up; only owld Peggy Hourihane within in the house and her daughter mindin' the child. Me father and mother is ded. I will go 'list for a sojer. God help us; these are bad times.

"Your faithful servant,

"PATRICK ROCHE."

On getting this letter, my father started at once for Ireland. I was at this time about a year old, a very ugly and stubborn little baby, so Aunt Jane has often told me; and when my mother held me high above the sunflowers at the gate, to kiss my hand to my father as he drove away, I only beat her upon the head and screamed for the pussy.

That was the last chance I ever had of seeing my father. He wrote to my mother from New York, and again from Queenstown—short dispirited letters ; the latter saying that he had caught a bad cold, and felt the change from a Californian to an Irish winter very severely. A week afterwards came another letter in a strange handwriting. It was from my Uncle Dominick, and it told my mother, not unkindly, the news that she never quite recovered from. The cold which my father had spoken of had turned to pleurisy, and he had died in a hotel in Queenstown the day after he landed. The writer said that, owing to the unfortunate relations that existed between him and his brother, he had not been aware of his marriage till letters that he had found in his possession informed him of the fact. He now forwarded them to her, with his brother's few

personal effects, and remained, hers faith-
fully, D. Sarsfield.

The next mail brought a second letter
from my Uncle Dominick. Since he last
wrote, my grandfather had died; and by
the terms of his will, in consequence of my
father having predeceased him, the property
and house of Durrus passed to the second
son, the writer himself. "Had my father
known that my brother had married,"
wrote my uncle, he might possibly have
made an alteration in the terms of the will;
but as Owen had never seen fit to make
any communication on the subject, no such
provision was made. The property has
suffered much during the recent famine,
but, as I feel sure that it would have
been in accordance with my father's wishes,
I have ventured to place a small sum to
your credit at the Bank of Ireland, with
directions to forward it to your order."

My mother never allowed the correspondence thus begun with my Uncle Dominick to drop altogether, and once or twice a year she would devote a couple of mornings to the toilful compilation of a letter to the brother-in-law whom she had never seen. Looking back now, I think there was something very touching in the confident way in which she relied on his interest in those annals of my childhood which filled her letters. I came upon them long afterwards, and read them with a strange mingling of feeling, very different from the wonder and longing with which I, in those childish days, saw them despatched on the first stage of their long journey, and wished that I could accompany them into the post-bag's grimy recesses, and go to Durrus too.

I had a very happy childhood. Either my mother or Uncle James could single-handed have spoiled the best of children, and their joint efforts being devoted to giving me everything I wished for, I should, had it not been for Aunt Jane, have lived a life of lawless enjoyment. The result of their long years of subjugation was a secret exultation in the undaunted front which I bore towards my aunt, and at a very early age I had learnt to recognize the fact that we three were confederates against a common despot. Uncle James was my most daring ally, and at his instigation I committed some of my most signal and spirited misdemeanours. By the time I was sixteen, I had become, under his supervision, a young lady of varied, if unusual, attainments. I could catch and saddle my own horse; I could guide a steam-plough; I could make some attempt at Latin verse; I knew a little about the rotation of crops, and a good deal of Shakespeare and Walter Scott. Aunt Jane herself took charge of my music, and I spent a daily hour of suffering at a piano as upright and unsympathetic as she was, learning from the frayed, discoloured pages of her music-books, the old-fashioned marches, and " Scotch airs with variations," that had formed the taste of two generations of Farquharsons.

I think my mother would have been satisfied to let me grow up as I was then doing, knowing nothing of the usual more elegant accomplishments of young ladies; and it was owing to Aunt Jane's abhorrence of my " tom-boy tricks" that the first great change in my life was made. The climax came one early summer morning, when, possessing myself of Uncle James's gun, I crept out to try and slay one of the big " jack-rabbits" that abounded on the ranch.

My aunt from her bedroom window saw

the whole performance—the stalking; the unseemly grovellings and crawlings through the long grass; the deliberate aim; and, finally, the stealthy but triumphant return with the spoil.

That very day it was decided that my mother and I were to go forthwith to Boston, there to abide with a cousin of my mother's, until such time as some of the high literary polish of that city should be imparted to me.

" Perhaps Rachel Campbell will be given patience to bear with her wild heathen-like ways," Aunt Jane had said; and my poor mother had answered with a sigh—

" Theo is always good to me, dear Jane; 'but I dare say you are right, and it will be best for us to go away."

So my mother and I set out on our long journey, little thinking that we should never see Farquharson's Ranch again.

Towards the end of our second year in Boston Uncle James died. His horse fell with him, throwing him on his head, and he only lived for a few hours afterwards, never recovering consciousness. He left all his property to my mother and my aunt; and the latter, having sold the ranch, came to live with us in Boston.

My uncle's death was the first trouble that I had ever known; but in the near future a still greater one awaited me. I was barely twenty-two when my mother's unexpected death seemed to bring the whole world to a standstill. I do not like to look back to the desolate days which followed. She was all I had in the world to love, and Aunt Jane's stern, undemonstrative nature would admit me to no fellowship of sorrow.

I dare say it may have been my own fault, but after a time I found the change from my mother's unexacting governance to Aunt Jane's rule becoming intolerable.

"Theodora has been quite ruined by poor Helen," she used, I believe, to say to her friends. "She will do nothing now but what is right in her own eyes. I shudder to think what will become of her."

Either my aunt's temper or mine had disimproved with advancing years, and each day I found it harder to avoid a breach of the peace. At length a diatribe upon "the fearful irreverence to my elders which I had learnt in this godless town," ending with reflections upon my mother's indulgence, aroused me to angry rejoinder.

I was trying to simmer down in my own room after the encounter, and in my stormy trampings to and fro in that limited apartment, I had twice upset a photograph of a plump and smiling little boy that stood on my table.

"That horrid little Willy Sarsfield!" I said, delighted to find something on which to expend my wrath; "he is always tumbling down!"

The picture had been my mother's, one which, at her request, had been sent to her by my Uncle Dominick many years before; and as for the second time I picked it up and put it in its place, an idea came to me.

"Why should I not go to Durrus?" I said.

I did not wait for a calmer moment, but, seating myself at the table, I immediately began a letter to my Uncle Dominick. My hand shook from the excitement of my suddenly taken resolution and from a sense of its temerity, but I was at least able to make my meaning clear. I had, I said, since I was a child, longed to visit Durrus, and see my father's relations; but hitherto this had been impossible to me. Now, however, I was comparatively alone in the world, and if my uncle would allow me to pay him a visit, nothing remained to prevent my doing so.

That evening I told my aunt of the step I had taken. The heat of her altercation with me had not yet died out in her, and, though she was, as she said, beyond measure astounded, her pride did not permit her to remonstrate.

"You can do as you please, Theodora. As your mother did not see fit to leave me the control of your fortune, I do not presume to give an opinion as to your movements. I trust, however, that you may not have cause to regret the head-strong self-will which has made you unable to content yourself in a quiet and God-fearing household."

During the days of waiting for an answer from my uncle, Aunt Jane preserved the same demeanour of distant disapproval, and I began to feel that to leave her house with the weight of her displeasure still hanging over me, would be a strong measure. The morning at length came on which I tore open an envelope with the Irish post-mark, and read to her the ceremonious letter in which Uncle Dominick intimated his and his son's great pleasure at the prospect of a visit from me.

"Very good; then I suppose you will start without delay." Her cold voice quavered unexpectedly at the end of the sentence, and, looking up in astonishment, I saw in her hard grey eyes an unmistakable moisture. "I had no wish to drive you out, Theodora."

"I know, Aunt Jane," I broke in, in hasty penitence; "I never thought that for an instant."

But she hurried away before I could get any further, saying inarticulately, as she left the room, "God bless you, child, wherever you go."

After this Aunt Jane made no further comment on what had taken place, but we found ourselves on a more friendly footing than we had ever been before; and when I said good-bye to her, I did so with the knowledge that I could always rely on her undemonstrative, but steadfast affection.

This is the history of how, on the 18th of October, 188–, I came to be reclining in a deck chair on board the s.s. *Alaska*, two hours from Queenstown.

CHAPTER III.

MY COUSIN WILLY.

"Willy's fair and Willy's rare,
And Willy's wondrous bonny."

"*To Miss Sarsfield, s.s. ' Alaska,' Queens-town. From W. Sarsfield.*

"Awfully sorry I will not be able to meet you. Drive to Foley's Hotel. Will be waiting you there."

This despatch was put into my hand before I left the steamer at Queenstown. Its genial tone and eccentric grammar were quite in keeping with my ideas of an Irishman. These were at once simple and

definite. All Irishmen were genial; most
of them were eccentric. In fact, had my
uncle and cousin met me on the pier, clad
in knee-breeches and tail-coats, and hailed
me with what I believed to be the national
salutation " Begorra! " I should scarcely
have been taken aback.

The outside car on which I drove from
the Cork station to the hotel was also
a realization of preconceived ideas. In
response to the bewildering proffers of
" Inside or outside ? " I had selected an
" outside," and was quite satisfied with the
genuineness of the difficulty I found in
remaining on it, as we rattled through the
muddy streets. The carman himself was
perhaps a little disappointing. His replies
to my questions were not only devoid of
that repartee which I had understood to be
the attribute of all Irish carmen, but were
lacking in common intelligence; and on

his replying for the third time, " Faith, I dunno, miss," I concluded I must have hit on an unlucky exception.

The day had lost none of the brilliancy of the early morning. It seemed to me that the sun shone with a deliberate intention of welcome, and the unfamiliar softness of Irish air was almost intoxicating. Everything was conspiring to put me into the highest spirits, and I only laughed when my new dressing-bag was flung on to the pavement by the dislocating jerk with which the car pulled up in front of Foley's Hotel.

As I walked into the hotel, the porter who had taken in my boxes, went over to a tall young man who was leaning over the bar at the end of the narrow hall, and whispered something to him. He immediately started from his lounging position, and, furtively glancing at the mirror behind the bar, he came up to me.

"How do you do? I'm very glad to see you over here," he said, with an evident effort to assume an easy cousinly manner. "I hope you didn't mind not meeting me. I was awfully sorry I couldn't get down to Queenstown, but I had important business in town." It was perhaps a consciousness of the interested scrutiny of the young lady behind the bar that caused him to blush an ingenuous red as he spoke. "You'd better come on and have some luncheon," he continued, without giving me time to answer him. "We've only got an hour before the train starts."

I followed him into the coffee-room, thinking as I did so how different this well-dressed, rather awkward young man was from the picturesque and vivacious creature I had somehow pictured my Irish cousin to be. His accent, however, was unmistakably that of his native country;

or, rather, as I afterwards found, that of his particular part of it. His quick, low way of speaking was at first a little unintelligible to me, and almost gave me the idea that what he said was intended to be of a confidential nature; but on the whole I thought his voice a singularly pleasant one, and listened with interest to its friendly modulations.

By the time our luncheon was put on the table he was more at his ease, and had even, with a sheepish, half-deprecating glance from his light grey eyes, addressed me as "Theo." The almost fraternal familiarity of the head waiter was, on Willy's explanation that I was his cousin from America, extended in the fullest degree to me.

"Indeed, when I seen her coming in the door, I remarked to Miss Foley how greatly the young lady favoured the

Sarsfield family," he observed blandly; " and Miss Foley said she considered she had a great likeness to yourself, captain."

This was a little embarrassing. I did not quite know what I was expected to say, and devoted myself to my mutton-chop.

" I did not know that you were a soldier," I said, as soon as the waiter had gone.

" Oh, well," replied my cousin, giving a conscious twist to his yellow moustache, " I'm only a sort of one—what they call ' a malicious man.' I'm a captain in the West Cork Artillery Militia," he explained; " but nobody calls me that but the buckeens hereabouts."

I wondered silently what a buckeen was, and why it should be so anxious to main-tain the prestige of the militia, but did not like to betray too much ignorance of what might be one of the interesting old courtesy titles peculiar to Ireland.

Looking at my cousin as he rapidly devoured his luncheon, I noticed that, in spite of his disclaimer of military rank, he took some pains to cultivate a martial appearance. His straw-coloured hair was clipped with merciless precision, and on his sunburnt forehead, what was evidently a cherished triangle of white marked the limit of protection afforded by an artillery forage cap.

"I think I'd better be looking after your luggage now," he said, bolting·what remained of his second chop, and getting up from the table with his mouth full. "I was quite frightened when I saw those two big mountains of trunks coming along on the car after you. And then when I saw *you* walk in "—he laughed a pleasant, foolish laugh—" I didn't think you'd be such a swell!" he ended, with confiding friendliness.

The terminus of the Cork and Moycullen railway, the line by which we were to travel to Durrus, was crowded on that Saturday afternoon. We had ten minutes to spare, during which I sat at the window and watched with the utmost interest the concourse on the platform. It had all the appearance of a large social gathering or conversazione. Stragglers wandered from group to group, showing an equal acquaintance with all, and with apparently entire nonchalance as to the functions of the train, while the guard himself bustled about among them with an interest that was evidently quite unofficial. My carriage soon became thronged with people, between whom and their friends on the platform a constant traffic in brown-paper parcels was carried on; and I was beginning to think there would be no room for Willy, who had disappeared in the crowd. But the ringing of the final bell set my mind at rest.

Contrary to the usual usage, this sound had the effect of almost emptying the train, and, the party in my carriage being reduced to two, I realized that the travellers were left in a minority by those who had come to bid them good-bye.

Willy returned at the last moment, emerging from the centre of a group of young ladies, with the well-pleased air of one whose conversation has been appreciated.

" Did you see those girls I was talking to ? " he said, as we moved out of the station. " They are cousins of the O'Neills, people in our part of the world. They came down to see me off. There was a great mob there to-day, but there always is on Saturday."

"Who are the O'Neills?" I asked, feeling that some response was expected of me.

"They're neighbours of ours. They live at Clashmore—that's four miles from us—and they're very nice people. Nugent, the brother, used to be a great pal of mine—at least, he was till he went to Cambridge, and came back thinking no one fit to speak to but himself."

Not feeling particularly interested in the O'Neills, I did not pursue the subject; but Willy was full of conversation.

"I'm just after buying a grand little mare in Cork. It was that kept me from going to meet you," he observed confidentially. "I suppose you learnt to ride at your ranch, Theo? I tell you what! I bought her for the governor, but she'd carry you flying, and you shall hunt her this winter if you like."

My cousinly feeling for Willy increased perceptibly at this suggestion.

" But," I said, " if your father buys her, he will want to ride her himself, won't he ? "

" Is it the governor ? "—with an intonation of contempt. " You never see *him* on a horse's back. He's always humbugging in the house over papers and books. I believe he used to be a great sportsman and fond of society, but he never goes anywhere now."

The two ladies who had started from Cork with us had got out a station or two afterwards, and we had the carriage to ourselves. But the extraordinary jolting and rattling of the train were not conducive to conversation, and, seeing that I was not inclined to talk, Willy relapsed into the collar of his ulster and the Cork newspaper, and ended by going unaffectedly to sleep.

It grew slowly darker. I sat watching the endless procession of small fields slipping past the window, until the grey monotony of colour made me dizzy. I leaned back, and, closing my eyes, tried to imagine the life I was going to, and to contrast its probabilities with my past experience. But a strange feeling of remoteness and unreality came upon me. I suppose that the mental exhaustion caused by so many new sights and impressions had dazed me, and I began to doubt that such a person as Theo Sarsfield had ever really existed. Willy, my Uncle Dominick, and my father flitted confusedly through my mind as inconsequently as people in a dream. I myself seemed to have lost touch with the world; my past life had slid away from me, and the future I had not yet grasped. I was a solitary and aimless unit in the dark whirl that surrounded me, and the sleeping figure at the opposite end of the carriage was a trick of imagination, and as unreal as I. I became more and more remote from things actual, and finally fell from all consciousness into a sleep as sound as Willy's.

My slumbers were at length penetrated by a shriek from the engine. I sat up, and saw that Willy was taking down his parcels from the rack; and in another minute we were in the little station of Moycullen.

A hat with a cockade appeared at the window.

" Hullo, Mick. Is it the dog-cart they've sent ? "

" 'Tis the shut carriage, Masther Willy," said Mick; " and 'tis waiting without in the street."

With some difficulty I followed Mick

through the crowd of carts in the station yard, to where a landau and pair **were** standing in the road. The moonlight **was** bright enough for me to see the fine shapes of the big brown horses, who were evincing so lively an interest in the movements of the engine that the coachman had plenty to do to keep them quiet.

"You're welcome, miss," said that functionary, touching his hat; and I got into the carriage, followed by Willy, with the usual number of impedimenta that appear necessary to male travelling youth.

"It's a good long drive," he said, arranging rugs over our knees—"twelve Irish miles. But we won't be very long getting there. You won't have time to be tired of me—I hope not, anyhow."

This was more like my idea of the typical Irishman, but was, nevertheless, rather discomposing from a comparative stranger. It was said, moreover, with a certain conquering air, which plainly showed that Willy was not accustomed to being found a bore. I could think of no very effective reply, so I laughed vaguely, and said I hoped I should not.

We had been driving at a good pace for about an hour, when we left the high-road and began the ascent of a long steep hill. At the top the carriage turned a sharp corner, and I saw below me, on my right, a great sheet of water all alight with the misty splendour of a full moon. Black points of land cut their way into the expanse of mellow silver, and the small islands were scattered like blots upon it.

"That's Roaring Water Bay," said Willy; "and that mountain over there's called Croagh Keenan"—pointing to a shadowy mass that formed the western limit of the bay. "You haven't anything to beat that in America, I'll bet!" An assertion which I refrained from combatting.

Our road now lay for a mile or two along the top of a hill overlooking the bay, and though Willy had done his best to make himself agreeable, I was tired enough to be extremely glad when the carriage swung sharply between high gate-posts, and we entered the avenue of Durrus.

As we passed the lodge, I caught, in the moonlight, a glimpse of the pretty face of a girl who opened the gates, and asked who she was.

"She's the lodgekeeper's daughter," said my cousin.

"She looked very pretty."

"Yes, she's not bad looking," he said indifferently. "There are plenty of good-looking girls in these parts."

The drive sloped down through a park

to the level of a turf bog, which it skirted for some distance, and then entered a thick clump of trees, through which the moonlight only penetrated sufficiently to let me see that they were growing in a species of reedy swamp, from which, on this cold night, a low frosty mist was rising. We were soon out again into the moonlight, the horses quickening up as they came near their journey's end. I saw a sudden gleam of sea in front, and on the left a long, low house, looking wan and ghostly in the moonlight.

CHAPTER IV.

THE MASTER OF DURRUS.

"My father's brother; but no more like my father
than I to Hercules."

As the carriage drew up at the hall door
it was opened by a stout elderly man, who
came forward with such empressement that
for a moment I thought it was my uncle.
Before, however, I had time to speak, he
said with much excitement—

"Your honour's welcome, Miss Sarsfield!"

Willy checked further remark on his
part by shovelling our many parcels into
his arms; but as soon as we had got into
the hall, he let them all go, and caught
hold of my hand and kissed it.

" Glory be to God that I should have lived to see this day ! I never thought I'd be bringing Masther Owen's child into this house. Thank God ! thank God ! "

" Come, Roche, that will do for a start," said Willy, laughing. " Keep the rest for another day. Here's the master."

Roche hastily let go my hand, as a tall bowed figure came across the hall to meet me.

" Well, my dear Theodora, so you have found your way at last to these western wilds," said my uncle, and kissed me on the forehead, taking both my hands in his as he did so.

His manner was an extreme contrast to Willy's affable familiarity, and I was struck by the absence of Irish accent in his voice, which had a mellifluous propriety of intonation.

He led me into the room he had just

left, a small library, and placed a chair for me in front of the fireplace.

"You must be cold after your long journey. Sit down and warm yourself," he said politely, adding another log to the furnace that was blazing in the old brass-mounted grate.

He rubbed his long white hands together and drew back, so as to let the light of the lamp fall on my face.

"And your—a—relatives in America—you left them quite well, I hope? I dare say they resent your desertion of them very bitterly?" He laughed a little.

I made some perfunctory reply, and sat warming one frozen foot after the other, while my uncle stood with his back to the lamp, and surveyed me with guarded intentness.

I had expected him to be perhaps formal. in an old-world, courteous way; but this

strained and glacial geniality was a very
different thing, and disconcerted me considerably.

"How unlike he is to Willy! I wish
he would not stare at me like that. I
don't think he is a bit glad to see me," I
thought, with hasty inconsequence. "Why
does he not speak? Well, I will," and I
made an ordinary remark about my journey.
My voice seemed to startle him from a
reverie. He put his hand to his eyes, and
made some alteration in the lamp before
replying.

It was a distinct relief when, at this
juncture, Willy came in, and offered to
show me the way to my room. We passed
through the dark entrance-hall, whose
depths were inadequately lighted by a
cheap lamp, its orange light forming a
dingy halo that contended hopelessly with
the surrounding gloom. At the end of

the hall was a broad flight of stairs, that at the first landing branched into two narrower flights leading to a corridor running round the hall. Passing along one side of this corridor, Willy opened a door at the end of it.

" Here you are," he said; " and I told them to bring you up a cup of tea; I thought you looked as if you wanted it "— with which he took his departure.

I was grateful for Willy's unexpected thoughtfulness in the matter of the tea. My uncle's reception had chilled me. I was tired by my long journey, and the darkness and silence of the house had a depressing effect upon my spirits. For weeks this arrival at Durrus had been constantly in my mind, and now that it was over, the only definite emotions it seemed to have produced were disappointment and dejection.

I looked round me as I sipped my tea, and did not feel enlivened by what I saw. The room was large and bare. The paper and the curtains of the two windows were alike detestable in colour and pattern. The enormous bed had once been a four-poster, but the posts had been cut down, and four meaningless stumps bore witness to the mutilation it had undergone. A colossal wardrobe loomed in a far-off corner; a round table of preposterous size occupied the centre of the room. Six persons could comfortably have dined at the dressing-table. In fact, the whole room appeared to have been fitted up for the reception of a giantess, and was quite out of proportion to my moderate stature of five feet seven.

I have always disliked more than one door in a bedroom, as it seems to me to afford to ghosts and burglars unnecessary facilities; and my dislike of my gaunt apartment reached its climax when I saw a door in the corner on the farther side of the fireplace from the door into the corridor. It had been papered over along with the walls, and its consequent unobtrusiveness had almost the effect of intentional concealment. I opened it, and found that it led into a moderate-sized bedroom. The moonlight which came through the uncurtained window lay in greenish-white patches on the uncarpeted floor, and showed a few pieces of furniture, shrouded in sheets and huddled in one corner. In spite of its chill bareness, an effect of recent occupancy was given to it by a chair that stood sideways in the window with an air of definiteness, and underneath and beside it I noticed a few tattered books.

I went back to my own room with an

unexplainable shudder, slamming the door
behind me, and proceeded to dress for
dinner with all speed.

With the unfailing punctuality of a new-
comer, I left my room as the gong sounded.
and, hurrying down, found my uncle and
Willy waiting for me in the library.

The dining-room was a large and im-
posing room. A moderate number of
portraits of the most orthodox ancestral
type hung, interspersed with mezzotints
of impassioned Irish clergymen, on its
panelled walls. A high old sideboard of
what seemed to me an unusual shape
stretched up to the ceiling on one side
of the room, and the plate upon it twinkled
in the blaze of the fire.

We sat down at the long table; and
while Willy and his father were absorbed
in overcoming the usual embarrassments
offered by soup to the wearers of mous-

taches, I amused myself with speculations as to who was responsible for the subtle combination of yellow and magenta dahlias that adorned the table. I concluded that the artist must have been the old butler, Roche; and as, at the thought, I involuntarily looked towards him, I found his eyes fixed upon me with the abstracted gaze of one who is trying to trace a likeness. Our eyes met, and he shuffled away, but I felt sure that he had been searching for a resemblance to the refined, well-cut, humorous face which, from a miniature of thirty years ago, I knew must be what he remembered of my father.

"It is quite an unusual pleasure to Willy and me to see a charming young lady at our bachelor-table—eh, Willy?" said Uncle Dominick, lifting his face from his now empty soup-plate, and smiling at me.

Willy, whose flow of language seemed

checked by his father's presence, gave an assenting grunt.

"It is a long time since there has been a Miss Sarsfield at Durrus, and it is thirty years since she died. You will find Willy and I are sad barbarians, and we shall have to trust to you to civilize us."

I am singularly unfitted to deal with the compliments of elderly gentlemen. On this occasion I failed as signally as usual to attain the requisite quality of playful confusion, and diverted the conversation by a question about a claret-coloured ancestor, who had been staring at me from his frame over the fireplace ever since we had sat down to dinner.

"That is my grandfather," said my uncle. "Dick the Drinker, they called him. He neither is nor was an ornament to the family; but his wife, the beautiful Kate Coppinger, is worth looking at. In fact, my dear"—with another smile and a little bow—"directly I saw you I was reminded of a miniature which we have of her."

"I hope she looks Irish," I responded. "I have always tried to live up to my idea of an Irish girl; but though my hair is dark, I haven't got violet eyes."

"No, nor any one else either. I never heard of them out of a book," said Willy, abruptly.

It was almost his first contribution to the conversation; but his father took no more notice of him than if he had not spoken, and went on eating his dinner, taking longer over each mouthful than any one I had ever seen.

"Then, am I not like the Sarsfields?" I asked.

My uncle paused and looked hard at me for a second or two, letting his heavy eyebrows drop over his eyes, with a peculiar change of expression.

"In some ways, perhaps," he said shortly. Then, turning to Willy, "Nugent O'Neill was here this afternoon to see you about the stopping of some earths. I told him to come over and dine here some day next week. Not "—turning to me—" that he is much of a ladies' man, but he is a gentlemanlike young fellow enough; very unlike his father," he added, in a bitter tone.

"Why, is Mr. O'Neill very objectionable?" I said.

I felt an unmistakable kick under the table, and Willy, with an admonitory wink, slurred over my question by saying—

"I can tell you, O'Neill would be pretty mad if he heard you calling him *Mr.* He's *The* O'Neill, and his wife's Madam

O'Neill, and they wouldn't call the queen their cousin."

My uncle silently continued his dinner, but I noticed how unpleasant his expression had become since The O'Neill was mentioned.

I finally made up my mind that his face was one I should never care for. He was decidedly a handsome man, though unusually old-looking for his age, which could not have been more than sixty.

His thick dark eyebrows lay like a bar across his high forehead. A long hooked nose drooped over an iron-grey moustache, which, when he smiled, lifted in a peculiar way, and showed long and slightly prominent yellow teeth. His unwholesomely pallid skin was deeply lined, and hung in folds under the dark sunken eyes, giving a look of age which was further contributed to by the stoop in his square shoulders. As I glanced from him to Willy, I concluded that the latter's blonde common-place good looks must have been inherited from his mother.

Rousing himself from the morose silence into which he had fallen, my uncle proceeded to apply himself to the task of entertaining me by a dissertation on the trade and agriculture of California. I soon found that he had all the desire to impart information which characterizes those whose knowledge of a subject is taken from pamphlets; but I listened with all politeness to his description of the country in which I had lived most of my life. Willy maintained a discreet silence, but from time to time bestowed on me glances of sympathy and approbation. Evidently Willy did not know how to talk to his father.

As dinner progressed, I observed that, if Roche allowed his master's glass to remain empty, he was at once given a sign to refill it, and my uncle became more and more diffusely instructive.

During dessert a pause at length gave me an opportunity of changing the conversation.

"I saw such a pretty girl at your gate lodge as we drove in," I said. "She looked delightful in the moonlight, with a shawl thrown over her head."

If Uncle Dominick had looked black at the mention of The O'Neill, he became doubly so at this apparently inoffensive remark. Glancing for explanation to Willy, I was amazed to see that he had become crimson, and was elaborately trying to show his want of interest in the subject by balancing a fork on the edge of his wine-glass.

"Yes," said my uncle; "she is a good-looking girl enough, and no one knows it better than she does. When people in that class of life are taken out of their proper place "—with great severity—" they at once begin to presume."

Willy upset his wine-glass with a sudden jerk. For my part, I was so taken aback by this tirade, that I thought my safest plan lay in immediate flight. Willy got up with alacrity, and, following me from the room, opened the drawing-room door. He looked confused and annoyed.

"Can you take care of yourself in there for a while?" he said. "I'll be with you in a few minutes."

CHAPTER V.

IMPRESSIONS.

" Groping in the windy stair,
    Darkness and the breath of space
    Like loud waters everywhere."

THE room was cold, and I at once made for
the fire, and, to my surprise, found the
hearthrug occupied by an untidy little girl,
who was engaged in dropping grease from
a candle over the coals to make them burn.
On seeing me she sprang to her feet, and,
with semi-articulate apologetic murmurs,
she gathered up a coal-box and retired in
confusion.

I concluded that, improbable as it

appeared, this was the under-housemaid, and reflected with some astonishment on the incongruities of the Durrus establishment. However, I afterwards found she held no official position, but was a satellite of the under-housemaid's, privately imported by her as a species of body-servant or slave. In fact, at the risk of digressing, I may here add that in process of time I discovered that the illicit apprenticeship of a young relation was a common custom of the Durrus servants, and in the labyrinthine remoteness of the servants' quarters they could be concealed without fear of attracting the master's eye.

In spite of its top dressing of grease, the fire was not a tempting one to sit over, and I roamed round the large ill-lighted room, taking in with leisurely wonderment the style of its decorations. It was, in startling contrast to the rest of the house, painted and papered in semi-æsthetic hues, pale sage-green and pink being the prevailing colours. This innovation of culture had not, however, extended itself to the furniture, which was of the solidly ugly type prevalent fifty years ago.

Heavy mahogany tables, each duly set forth with books and daguerrotypes, stood inconveniently about, causing a congestion among the lesser furniture. The pictures, which had been taken down at the re-papering of the room, leaned against the wall with their faces inwards. I turned one of the nearest to me, expecting to come upon a family portrait, but found it represented a Turk of truculent aspect, worked in Berlin wool—a testimony to the amount of spare time at the disposal of the ladies of Durrus. The thick coating of dust on my fingers which was the result of this investigation did not encourage me to make any further researches, and an examination of the old china on the marble cheffonier between the windows had equally disastrous results. In one corner there was an ancient grand piano, which to my astonishment proved to be in good tune. I had not been playing for very long when Willy came in, and, without speaking, placed himself beside me.

"Well, I declare!" he said, as I finished playing one of Schubert's impromptus, "it's a long, time since I heard that old piano. I got it tuned the other day on purpose for you, and you know how to knock sparks out of it, anyhow! I heard Henrietta O'Neill playing that piece once, and it didn't sound half so well—though, I can tell you, she thinks no end of herself."

"By-the-by, Willy, why did you stop me when I began to speak of Mr. O'Neill?"

"O'Neill," corrected Willy.

" Oh, well, *O'Neill*," I said peevishly. " But what was the harm of talking about him ? "

" No harm, as far as I am concerned, but the governor hates him like poison. I believe they had some row in my grandfather's time—I don't know exactly what —and they never made it up since. But there's no regular quarrel; I go to all their parties, and I think the governor rather likes Nugent and the girls."

" What is Madam O'Neill like ? "

" Oh, *I* get along with her first-rate," said Willy, stretching out one of his long legs, and serenely studying the gold-embroidered clock on his sock. " But other people say she's rather a bitter old pill; and I can tell you, she has the two girls in great order ! "

I began to play as he finished speaking; but his thoughts had travelled on to my other unlucky remark at dinner, for he presently interrupted me by saying in an uncertain way—

"Oh! you know that girl we were talking of at dinner, the one you saw at the gate—Anstice Brian her name is—her mother is a bit queer in her head, and she'd be very apt to give you a start if you didn't know her ways. She's a harmless poor creature, but she wanders about these bright nights, and she gets into the house sometimes."

I probably looked as alarmed as I felt, for he laughed protectingly, and, drawing his chair a little closer to mine, said reassuringly—

"Never fear! She's not half as silly as they say; and do you think I'd let her be about if there was any chance at all of her frightening you?"

"What is she like? Is she an old

woman ? " — ignoring the reproachful warmth of this last observation.

" Is it old Moll Hourihane ? She's as old as two men—or she looks it, anyhow. She used to be my nurse till she went off her head."

" I thought you said her name was Brian," I said.

" That's only her husband's name. The women mostly stick to their own names in this country when they're married."

" And you're quite sure she's not dangerous ? " I said, feeling only half reassured.

" No more than I am myself"—with a glance to see if I were going to contradict this assertion. " She has a sort of dumb madness—like a hound, you know—and she'll never speak ; though I dare say after all that's no great loss," he concluded.

I was by this time feeling very sleepy, and hoping I should soon be able to escape to my own room, when the door opened, and my uncle came solemnly in.

"I have come, Theodora, my dear, to suggest an early retirement on your part."

He avoided looking at Willy, and I felt that the effects of my ill-timed remarks at dinner had not yet died out. He looked haggard and troubled, and a sudden pity and sense of kinship impelled me to raise my cheek towards him as he took my hand to say good night. He stooped his head as if to kiss me, but checked himself, and after an instant of hesitation his moustache touched my forehead.

There was something repelling in his manner, but I felt that he was not unconscious of the sympathy I had intended to express. He turned and left the room, and I heard him go back to the library and shut himself in, the sound of the closing door emphasizing his solitariness.

I went upstairs with the feeling of isolation again strongly upon me. The wind had risen, and on the walls of the draughty corridor each gust made the old pictures shake in their mouldering frames. At intervals, through the panes of the large skylight overhead, the moon's light dropped in pale wavering squares on the floor of the hall below. I leaned over the balustrades watching the spectral alternations of light and darkness, as the clouds swept across the moon, till the objects beneath me seemed to take intermitting motion from the flitting of the moonbeams.

As I looked, the dim lamp in the hall flickered and went out. A gust from below circled round the corridor, lifting the hair upon my forehead and almost extinguishing my candle as it passed me.

Perhaps I was overtired and nervous, but a causeless fear possessed me—the old unreasoning dread of some vague pursuit out of the darkness, that I had not felt since I was a child. I gave a terrified glance over my shoulder at the swaying pictures, and then, shielding my candle with my hand, I ignominiously ran down the corridor into my own room.

CHAPTER VI.

AN IRISH SUNDAY.

" In Islington there was a man,
    Of whom the world might say,
That still a godly race he ran,
    Whene'er he went to pray."

" WILL you have your tay, plase, miss ? "

The words at first mingled with the dreams which had all night disturbed my sleep. On being repeated, the unfamiliar accent, accompanied by the clink of a cup and saucer, made me open my eyes. A pleasant-looking, red-haired girl was standing by my bed, tray in hand.

" You're after having a great sleep, miss. I was twice here before, and there wasn't a stir out of you."

"Is it very late?" I asked, with an alarming recollection of my uncle's punctuality.

"Oh, not at all, miss. The masther's only just after having his breakfast."

"What!" I gasped. "You should have called me earlier."

" Oh, there's no hurry, miss! Sure he always ates his breakfast by himself, and there's no sayin' how late it'll be before Masther Willy's down."

Calmed by this assurance, I did not hurry myself over my dressing, but from time to time stopped to look at the view from my windows.

It was a quiet October day, with a grey yet luminous sky, that lit with a grave radiance the group of yellow elms that divided the avenue from a heathery expanse of turf-bog, with low hills beyond. From the other window, which was almost over the hall door, I could see to the left a dark belt of trees that went round to the back of the house; and in front, at the foot of the lawn, the curve of a little bay. This was separated from the larger waters of Durrusmore Harbour by a low promontory, along whose ridge a meagre line of fir trees was etched against the grey sky. Leaning out of the window, and looking westwards towards the mouth of the harbour, I saw the Atlantic lying broad and white under the light of the soft clear morning.

I went downstairs, and as I passed along the corridor, I felt, even on this still day, the air circulating freely through broken panes in the skylight and the staircase window, making it easy to account for the ghostly eddyings of the wind the night before.

Willy had apparently made an effort on my behalf at early rising, and I found him making tea when I came into the dining-room. He came forward to meet me with a complacency in which I detected a consciousness of the added smartness of his Sunday attire; and, having satisfactorily ascertained the fact that I had slept well, he installed me behind the urn to pour out the superfluously strong tea which he had just brewed.

I experienced undeniable relief in the absence of Uncle Dominick, whom at this moment I saw pacing up and down a walk leading from the house to the sea. Willy saw the direction of my eyes.

"I hope you're not insulted by only me breakfasting with you," he said, with un-grammatical gallantry. "You can breakfast with the governor whenever you like, but you will have to be down at eight o'clock to do that!"

I intimated with fitting politeness that I was satisfied with the present arrangement, and we began our *tête-à-tête* meal in great amity. Willy, indeed, was an excellent host. He plied me with everything on the table, eating his own breakfast and talking all the time with unaffected zest and vigour, and I began to feel as if the time I had known him could be reckoned in months instead of hours.

The necessity of writing to announce my safe arrival to Aunt Jane was one that had already forced itself upon my notice.

"I thought you'd be wanting to write a letter," Willy said, conducting me into the drawing-room after breakfast, " and I got the place ready for you."

I sat down at the old-fashioned writing-table, and found that he had anticipated my wants with a lavish hand. Through the window I saw him, a few minutes afterwards, sauntering down the drive towards the lodge, smoking a cigarette, with two little white dogs flashing in circles round him; and as I watched him, I came to the conclusion that at first sight I had underestimated my cousin.

There was something to me half amusing and half touching in the anxiety of his little housewifely attentions to me. He was really unusually thoughtful for others; from various things he had said, it was evident that his father had allowed the whole management of the place to devolve on him, and I fell to idle speculation as to whether he ordered dinner, and if he were particular about the housemaids wearing white muslin caps; and I was only aroused from these, and other equally interesting reflections by hearing the clock strike the hour at which I had been warned I must get ready for church.

My uncle was standing on the steps, with his Prayer-book in his hand, when I came downstairs. He wished me good morning, with a polite apology for not having met me at breakfast, and stood looking about him, with eyelids narrowed by the white glare from the sea, till a minute afterwards the wagonnette in which we were going to church came to the door. My uncle and I got in behind; while Willy, with Mick by his side, sat on the box and drove. Once outside the gate, we took a road running at right angles to that by which I had arrived. It went round the head of Durrusmore Harbour, and, leaving the sea behind, turned inland through large woods, which my uncle told me were part of the demesne of Clashmore, The O'Neill's place.

The road was level, and soft with the fallen red beech leaves, and the brown horses took us along it at a pace that showed they were none the worse for their journey the night before. The rough stone walls on either side of the road were covered with moss and small ferns. Here and there the wood was pierced by narrow rides—vistas in which the clumps of withering bracken repeated the brown and gold of the trees above.

" We're going to draw this place on Friday," said Willy, pausing in the steady flow of his conversation with Mick to give me the information. " Blackthorn will carry Miss Theo right enough, wouldn't he, Mick? and I'll ride the new mare."

The village of Rathbarry, which we had now entered, consisted of a single street of low, dirty-looking cottages, their squalid uniformity varied at frequent intervals by the more prosperous shuttered face of a public-house. At the end of the street, a gateway led into a graveyard, surrounded by ill-thriven elm trees, in the middle of which stood the church. It was an ugly, oblong building, with a square tower at the west end, from which proceeded a clanging as of a cracked basin battered with a spoon.

"We're in good time," said Willy, drawing up with a flourish before the porch. "That's the hurry-bell only begun now, so we've five minutes to spare. Look, Theo! there's the Clashmore carriage. Did you ever see such brutes as those chestnuts?"

Before, however, I had time to reply, Uncle Dominick hurried me into the church, and we took our places in opposite corners of a singularly uncomfortable square pew. As we sat confronting each other in the half-empty church, we heard in the porch Willy's voice raised in agreeable converse. Apparently his remarks were of a complimentary sort, for a girl's voice rejoined, " Oh, nonsense, Willy ! " with a laugh.

" Disgraceful ! " muttered my uncle, under his breath ; and the next moment three ladies swept up the aisle, followed by Willy, on whose face still beamed a slightly fatuous smile.

He immediately sat down beside me, and in a rapid whisper instructed me as to the more prominent members of the congregation.

" Those are the O'Neills "—indicating the ladies he had come in with. " Connie's the little fair one. And look ! those are the Jackson Crolys ! You'd better sit up and behave, as they'll be watching you all the time. I know they all want to see what you're like!"

"Hush! don't talk!" I whispered back. "Here's the clergyman."

The service was very long. The music, which consisted of the clergyman's daughter accompanying herself on a harmonium, with casual vocal assistance from a couple of school-children, was of an unexhilarating kind. Willy fidgeted, admired his boots, trimmed his nails, and tried to utilize every possible opening for conversation. Uncle Dominick, on the contrary, devoted his whole attention to the service, and answered all the responses with austere punctilious-ness, even going so far as to try and track the clergyman's daughter in her devious course through the hymns.

From the corner which had been allotted to me in my uncle's pew I could not see the clergyman, and, though his voice resounded through the church, his very pronounced Cork accent made it difficult for me to understand more than a word here and there in his discourse.

The high sides of the pew debarred me from even the solace of inspecting the congregation, and, in the absence of other occupation, I could not altogether conceal the interest that I felt in the remark which Willy was laboriously spelling on his fingers for my edification. Becoming conscious, however, that Uncle Dominick's eye, while fixed upon the preacher, had included us in its observations, I transferred my attention to the mural tablets, which on either side of the church set forth the perfections of dead-and-gone O'Neills and Sarsfields.

Having studied these for a few minutes with the mild sceptical interest usually excited by the tabulated virtues of the unknown departed, I leaned back in my corner, and, in doing so, noticed a brass upon the wall slightly behind my uncle's seat. My eye was immediately caught by my father's name.

IN MEMORIAM.

THEODORE WILLIAM SARSFIELD,

WHO DEPARTED THIS LIFE

JANUARY 10, 185–.

AND OF

OWEN SARSFIELD,

SON OF THE ABOVE,

WHO DIED SUDDENLY IN CORK,

ON HIS RETURN FROM AMERICA,

JANUARY 9, 185–.

———

THIS MONUMENT IS ERECTED BY THEIR SORROWING SON
AND BROTHER, DOMINICK SARSFIELD, OF DURRUS.

I glanced by a natural transition to my uncle, whose head all but intervened between me and the brass. His expression of sombre melancholy harmonized well with the words " his sorrowing brother."

I could guess what must have been his grief at the death of an only brother, from whom he had been perforce alienated. Till then I had scarcely realized how closely linked their lives must once have been, and I resolved that his chilly manner should not deter me from some day inducing him to speak to me of my father.

As I made up my mind to this, the clergyman's voice ceased, and the congregation rose at the end of the sermon. We walked out of church close behind the O'Neills, and outside the porch Madam O'Neill stopped to shake hands with my uncle. Then, turning to me—

" I need not ask to be introduced to you, my dear. I knew your poor father very well indeed in days gone by." This was said in a dry attenuated voice, but through the elaborate pattern of her Maltese lace veil, her eyes looked kindly at me. She was small and refined looking, with little artificial airs and graces which told that she had been a beauty in her day; and what remained of a delicate complexion was carefully sheltered from the harmless light of the grey sky by a thick parasol.

Uncle Dominick's impatience to get away only gave me time to say a word or two in answer to her salutation.

"Come, Theodora," he said, with the smile that lifted his moustache and showed all his teeth. "We must not keep the horses waiting;" and bidding the madam and her two daughters, who had been standing behind her, good-bye, he led the way down to the gate.

Willy was already on the box of the wagonnette, and was talking to a dark, quiet-looking young man who was standing with one foot on the wheel.

"Then you'll see about having those earths stopped," Willy said, leaning over, and emphasizing what he was saying with the handle of the whip on his hearer's shoulder. "Oh, here they are! Theo, let me introduce Mr. O'Neill. I was just telling him he must be sure and have a fox for you at Clashmore this week."

"I shall do my best," said Mr. O'Neill, as he took off his hat; but he did not look particularly enthusiastic as he spoke.

We had no sooner driven off, than Willy twisted round on the box to speak to me.

"Well, what do you think of Nugent?" he said rather eagerly.

"He is nice looking," I replied critically; "but I do not like his expression. I cannot say he is what I should call either cheerful or agreeable looking."

"Oh, he's not half a bad chap," said Willy, with a leniency which was possibly the result of the pleasure with which young men listen to the depreciation of their fellows. "He's jolly enough sometimes; but he can put on a bit of side when he likes, and I dare say he thinks he is thrown away down here. Henrietta's like him in that sort of way, but Connie has no nonsense about her."

I decided that Connie's was the laugh that I had heard in the porch before service, and thought that of the two I should be more likely to prefer Henrietta.

Ever since we had left church the sky had been darkening, and when we reached Durrusmore Harbour, the distant headlands were almost hidden in a white mist. The south-west wind blew it towards us from the sea, and by the time we got home a thick fine rain was coming steadily down.

Lunch, with Uncle Dominick at the head of the table, was a more serious business than breakfast had been, and old Roche's shuffling ministrations added to the general solemnity. I was, however, amused by the affectionate solicitude with which he nudged me in the elbow with the dish of potatoes, indicating with his thumb a specially floury one, and concluded that this was the singular method he took of showing that his regard for my father had extended itself to me.

When lunch was over Willy announced his intention of walking to Clashmore, to see about borrowing a side-saddle for me, he said—an act of self-sacrifice which I was not slow to attribute to the fascinations of Miss Connie O'Neill. Uncle Dominick retired to a private den at the end of a dark passage leading from the hall to the back of the house; and a few minutes later,

Willy, in a voluminous mackintosh, set forth on his errand, followed by the fox terriers in a state of amiable frenzy, the result of the abhorred Sunday morning incarceration. I became aware that I was thrown upon my own resources, and, with the prospect of a wet afternoon before me, I felt my spirits sinking perceptibly.

To finish my letter to Aunt Jane was at least better than doing nothing. I took up a strong position in front of the library fire, and disconsolately applied myself to filling the big sheet of foreign paper on which I had embarked in the morning.

CHAPTER VII.

MOLL.

" Or in the night, imagining some fear,
How easy is a bush suppos'd a bear!"

WILLY did not come home till dinner-time, when he reappeared in exceedingly good humour. I, on the contrary, felt the vague ill-temper of a person who has spent a wet Sunday afternoon in solitude, and I found dinner long and dull. In the drawing-room after dinner, I sought the resource of music to raise my spirits; but I was debarred from even this last consolation, for Willy implored me to "let the piano alone," as his father disapproved of music on Sunday.

We finally settled down in armchairs by the fire, and I discovered that Willy possessed in a high degree the feminine faculty of sitting over a fire and talking about nothing in particular. He pretended to no superiority to the minor gossip which forms the ripples in the current of country life, and he had quite a special gift of recounting small facts with accuracy and detail, and without any endeavour to exalt his talent as a story-teller. His tales had, in consequence, a certain intrinsic freshness and merit, and till bedtime we maintained a desultory, but on the whole interesting conversation.

When I got up to my room, I found it full of smoke and extremely cold. The window had been opened to let out the smoke, and the chintz curtains rustled and flapped in the draught. Making up my mind after a few minutes that even turf smoke was preferable to the cold disquiet of the wind, I went to the window to close it, and noticed with a good deal of amusement that, the pulley being broken, the housemaid had supported the sash with one of my brushes.

There was something in this misplaced ingenuity which was eminently characteristic of the slipshod manner of life at Durrus, and by force of contrast my thoughts travelled back to my mother's orderly household. I leaned against the shutter and looked out, beset by poignant recollections of a time when life without my mother seemed an impossibility, and when Durrus was no more to me than a place in a fairy story.

The wind had blown away most of the fog, and the rain had ceased, but a thin haze still blunted the keenness of the moonlight. I gazed at the dark shapes of the trees in the shrubbery till I lost the sense of their reality, and they came and went like dreams in the uncertain light. In my ears was still the throb and tremor which seven days and nights spent in listening to the screw of the *Alaska* had imprinted on my brain, and my thoughts and surroundings seemed alike hurrying on in time to its pulsations. I was at length roused to realities by a sound which at first seemed part of the light chafing of the laurel leaves, but which in a few moments became detached and distinct from the vague noises of the autumn night.

It came nearer, and gave the impression of some stealthy advance in the wet grass under the trees. At length, at the verge of their shadow, just opposite my window, I heard the gravel crunch under a soft footstep. The next instant a woman's figure slid into the dim light, and came out across the broad gravel sweep with a rhythmical swaying gait, as though moving to music.

Half-way to the house she stopped, and, raising her arms above her head with a wild gesture, she began to step to and fro with jaunty liftings and bendings of her body, as though she were taking part in a dance. Backwards and forwards she paced with measured precision ; then, placing her hands on her hips, she danced with fantastic lightness and vigour some steps of an Irish jig. Suddenly, however, she checked herself ; she knelt down, and, turning a pale face to the sky, she crossed her hands on her breast and remained motionless.

Her absolute stillness had in it an intensity almost more dreadful than the strange movements she had previously gone through, and I stood staring in inert terror at the grey kneeling figure, with a face as white as that which was still turned rigidly skywards in what appeared to be the extremity of supplication. Just then the moon shone sharply out, hardening and fixing in a moment the limits of light and darkness, and, as if with a sudden movement, it flung the shadow of the praying woman on the ground before her. She started, and slowly rose to her feet, and, with her hands still crossed on her bosom, turned her face towards me. I saw the moonlight glisten in her wide-open eyes, which were fixed, not on me, but on the window of the room next to mine. Then opening her arms wide, she let them fall to her side with an extravagant obeisance, and sidled back into the impenetrable shadow of the trees.

There was I know not what unearthly

suggestion about this weird dance and agonized devotion, that seemed to paralyze my mind, and render it incapable of any thought except fear. I stood bewilderedly looking at the spot where the darkness had swallowed up her figure; but before I had time to collect my ideas, she reappeared at a little distance, and, as well as I could see, turned up a path which led through the shrubbery in the direction of the lodge.

As she passed out of sight, I suddenly remembered what Willy had said to me about Anstey's half-witted mother. This strange dancer was, then, no ghost nor dream-creature, sent on a special errand to me, as I had first feared, and then, with returning courage, had almost hoped might be the case.

She was only " old Moll Hourihane." It was a simple explanation, and perhaps a humiliating one; but, in spite of my anxiety to possess a ghost-story of my own, I accepted it with relief. I shut the window and locked my door, and, though still trembling all over with cold and excite-ment, I went to bed, thankful that "Mad Moll" had introduced herself to me from without, instead of first appearing to me within the walls of Durrus.

CHAPTER VIII.

SCHOOLING.

" Rode he on Barbary?   Tell me, gentle friend,
    How went he under him?"

" This is the prettiest low-born lass——"

" AND so she gave you a great fright?
Well, now, wasn't that too bad?   I wish
I'd caught her at her tricks, and I'd soon
have packed her about her business.   You
know, they say she was the best step-
dancer in the country when she was a
girl; and to think of her going dancing
under your window, and you taking her
for a ghost!"

Willy's amusement overcame his sympathy, and he laughed loud and long.

I had been impelled to confide my alarm of Sunday night to him when we were on our way round to the stables to see the horses, on the following morning, and I now rather resented his refusal to see anything but the ludicrous side of the incident.

"You are very unsympathetic. I am sure you would have been just as frightened as I was," I said. "She looked exactly like a ghost; and in any case I should like to know why she selected *my* window to dance under?"

"She meant it for a compliment, of course. I suppose she thought you'd be a good audience. *I*'ve seen her now and again jack-acting there in front of the house, but I'm afraid all I said was to tell her go home. But then, I'm not sympathetic like you!"

We had stopped to discuss the point at the spot whence I had seen Moll emerge, and now walked on past the untidy old flower-garden to the yard.

It was a large square, of which three sides were formed by stables and cowhouses, the house itself being the fourth, and was only redeemed from absolute ugliness by a row of four great horse-chestnut trees, which grew out of a grassy mound in the middle. We arrived in time to surprise the two little fox terriers, Pat and Jinny, in the clandestine enjoyment of a meal with the pig, whose trough was conveniently placed by the scullery door. On seeing us, they at once endeavoured to dissemble their guilty confusion by an unworthy attack on their late entertainer. This histrionic display did not, however, deceive Willy in the least. The dogs were ignominiously called off, and the pig was left master of the situation.

I wondered, as I looked round, if all Irish yards were like this one. Certainly I had never before seen anything like the mixture of prosperity and dilapidation in these solid stone buildings, with their ricketty doors and broken windows. Through the open coach-house door I saw an unusual amount of carriages, foremost among them the landau in which I had driven from Moycullen, with a bucket placed on its coach-box in order to catch a drip from the roof. A donkey and a couple of calves were roaming placidly about, and, though there was evidently no lack of stable-helpers and hangers-on, everything was inconceivably dirty and untidy.

The horses were, however, well housed and cared for. My future mount, " Black-thorn," was the first to be displayed. He was a big black horse, with an arched back and an ugly head; but he had a look of power and intelligence which provided me with materials for a sufficiently laudatory criticism. In the next box, the bay mare Willy had bought in Cork was pushing her nose through the bars over the door to attract our attention.

"That's the one kept me from going to meet you at Queenstown," said Willy, opening the door, and catching the mare by the head. "She's a nice little thing, but I'll know better another time than to throw you over for her. Stand, mare!"—as that animal made a vigorous remonstrance at being deprived of her sheet.

"She looks as if she knows how to go," I said. "What are you going to call her?"

"Don't you think you might christen her for me?" Willy answered, with an insinuating glance at me from under his black eyelashes. " Just to show you don't bear malice for my leaving you to cross Cork all alone."

Notwithstanding the access of brogue with which this was said, there was something in the look which accompanied it at which, to my extreme annoyance, I felt my colour rise.

" Of course I don't bear malice. I never even expected you to meet me," I said, turning to stroke the mare's shoulder. " If you really want a name for her, suppose you call her ' Alaska.' That was the steamer I came over in, and they say she's the fastest on the line."

Willy received this moderate suggestion with enthusiasm. " If she turns out half as good as she looks," he said, as we walked out of the yard, " you shall have her for yourself to ride."

" I think you are very rash to put me

up on your horses when you don't in the least know how I can ride."

"Ah! well, I'll trust you; though, indeed, after the funk you were put into by poor old Moll, I suppose I may expect to see you turning back at the first fence."

To this sally I vouchsafed no reply.

"I must take the mare out this afternoon," he continued, "to try can she jump. Blackthorn wants shoeing, or you should ride him; but I thought perhaps you'd like to walk up to the farm to see me schooling the mare. It's only as far as those fields opposite the lodge that I'll go."

This was, I thought, a very good suggestion. A prospective day with the hounds made me anxious to see what Irish fences were like, and we settled to start early in the afternoon.

At lunch Uncle Dominick was more conversational than I had yet seen him.

" What have you been doing with yourself this morning, Theo, my dear?"—for the first time adopting the more familiar form of my name. "The roses in your cheeks do credit to our Irish air."

Uncle Dominick's faded gallantry always had the effect of making me shy and constrained. I laughed nervously, and before I could reply Willy struck in—

" She was round to the stables with me, sir."

" Oho! so that was it, was it?" said my uncle, with the smile I disliked so much; and I felt that at that moment my cheeks more resembled peonies than roses.

" I was showing her the new mare," said Willy, "and we're going to call her ' Alaska,' because that's the ship that "—here he stopped—" because that's the fastest ship between this and America."

" Why, is not that the vessel that

brought you to us from America?" said Uncle Dominick, pursuing his advantage with unexpected facetiousness. "I think it is an admirable name, and will always have pleasant associations for you and me, eh, Willy?"

Willy made no reply, and my uncle rose from the table, apparently well satisfied with himself, and left the room humming a tune.

It was a softly brilliant afternoon. I thought, as I started for the farm where I was to see Alaska put through her paces, that I had never, even in America, seen anything like the glow of the yellow leaves against the blue sky—a blue so intense that it seemed to press through the half-stripped branches. The thick drifts of fallen leaves rustled like water about my feet, and floated on the surface of the pools which the rain of yesterday had formed in

the low swampy ground under the clump
of elms at the bend of the avenue. Just
here a deep dyke ran parallel with the
drive, separating it from the turf bog
which I had seen from my bedroom window.
Across it was a rough bridge of logs, from
which a raised cart-track wound over the
bog like a long brown serpent. I crossed
the bridge and leaned upon the rusty iron
gate that closed the approach to the bog
road. The keen scent of the sea came to
me across the heathery expanse, mingled
with the pure perfume of the peat, and I
regretted that my promise to Willy prevented me from following the meandering
course of the cart-track over the headland,
to where I heard the hollow draw of the
sea on the rocks at the other side.

Retracing my steps, I went up the
avenue, and found Willy with the two
dogs waiting for me outside the gate. In

the fence on the other side of the road was an opening partially filled by a low wall of loose stones—locally called a gap.

" I'll take her in at this gap," Willy said, turning the mare to give her room, and then putting her at the gap. Alaska, however, had probably her own reasons for preferring the road, for she refused with a vicious swerve, and a lively contest between her and her rider ensued.

The latter's difficulties were considerably complicated by Pat and Jinny, who, with ostentatious activity, insisted on crossing and recrossing the gap at the most critical moments. When Jinny at length took up a commanding position on its topmost stone, in order to watch, with palpitating interest and ejaculatory yelps, Alaska's misbehaviour, Willy's temper gave way.

" Theo," he said, with suppressed fury,

"will you for goodness' sake take that—that *infernal* dog out of my way?"

I captured Jinny, and held her wriggling in my arms, until at length Alaska, with a bound that would have cleared a five-barred gate, went into the field.

I climbed on to a gate-post, from whence I could conveniently see the schooling process. Willy was a fine rider, and Alaska acquitted herself very creditably; but after a quarter of an hour spent on my gate-post, I began to find it rather cold, and, Willy having gone to more distant fields in search of further educational difficulties, I decided to go home without him. Outside the gates was a large gravel sweep, with high flanking walls, forming a semicircular approach, and in these, at some height from the ground, several niches had been made, large enough to hold life-sized figures. As I turned to get down, I saw that a young girl was standing in one of the niches. She was leaning slightly forward, steadying herself with one hand on the wall, while with the other she shaded her eyes, as if looking after Willy's departing figure.

On seeing me, she jumped quickly down, and ran to open one of the small gates. I recognized the shy, pretty face of Anstey Brian, and stopped inside the gate to speak to her.

"If Mr. Sarsfield comes, will you tell him I have gone home?" I said; and was turning away, when Anstey, with a nervous blush, said, in a soft, deprecating voice—

"Oh, miss, I beg your pardon! I was very sorry to hear you got anny sort of a fright from my mother last night. It's just a little restless she is, those last few nights, and my father'd be greatly vexed if he thought you got anny annoyance by her."

I assured her that my alarm had only been momentary, wondering vaguely how she had heard anything about it.

"Indeed, miss, she'd hurt no one. She's this way, foolish-like, this long time."

"How long is it since it began?" I said, with interest.

"I never remember her anny other way, miss, though my father says she was once a fine, handsome girl, and as sensible as yourself, miss."

"Did her mind go from an accident?" I asked.

"Why, then, indeed, miss, I don't rightly know. She had some strange turn in her always, and afther I was born she got quare altogether; and that's the way she is ever since. Dumb, like she couldn't spake, and silly in her mind."

I was looking in the direction of the lodge while she spoke, half unconsciously noting how thickly the ivy trails hung over its small windows, when I became aware of a face looking out at me through one of them.

I could distinguish little of it beyond the wide-open, pale eyes, which were fixed upon me with a concentrated, half-terrified intentness; but with a momentary return of last night's unreasoning panic, I knew it to be the face of the woman of whom we were speaking. Something of this must have been shown in my expression, for Anstey, following the direction of my eyes, said—

" Don't be frightened at all, miss. Sure that's only poor mother. Will I bring her out here for your honour to see ? "

But I had no wish for any close acquaintance, so hastily saying that, as it was already dark, I had no time to stay, I wished Anstey good night.

I must confess that, as I walked away from the lodge, I was haunted by the frightened glare of Moll Hourihane's eyes. There had been something in their expression which, beneath the oblivion of insanity, seemed almost to struggle into recognition. At the remembrance of them, I felt the same unconquerable dread creep over me again, and I hurried along the avenue towards home. To my imagination, the patches of grey lichen on the trees repeated in the growing twilight the effect of the grey face at the darkened window. The dead leaves awoke as I trod on them, and followed me with whisperings and cracklings. It was a relief to leave the little wood behind, and to see in the library windows the flickering glow which told of a good fire, and suggested tea.

I was surprised and annoyed by the unwonted nervousness which had lately affected me. I prided myself upon being a singularly practical, unimaginative person; and yet now, for the third time since my arrival at Durrus, my self-possession had been disturbed by a trivial event, which I should formerly have laughed at. I walked rapidly to the house, determined for the future to give no toleration to my foolish fancy, and to——

"Here you are!" said Willy's voice from the hall door. "Come on and have some tea."

CHAPTER IX.

"*Ford.* Old woman! What old woman's that?

. . . . . .

A witch, a quean, an old cozening quean!
Have I not forbid her my house?"

IT occurred to me several times during the
next few days, how strangely little I saw
of my uncle. Except at luncheon and
dinner, he seldom or never appeared, even
in the evenings preferring to sit alone over
his wine in the gloomy dining-room, while
Willy and I were in the drawing-room.
At ten o'clock regularly the door would
open, and his tall austere figure would

appear, holding my candle ready lighted; and with the same little speech about the advantages of early hours for young people, he would wish me good night, politely standing at the foot of the stairs as I went up. As a rule, I did not see him again until luncheon next day, and I wondered more and more how he spent his time.

Willy seemed to know little more about his father's occupations than I did.

"Oh, *I* don't know what he's up to," he had said, when I asked him. "He prowls about the place from goodness knows what awful hour in the morning till breakfast, and he sits in that den of his all day, more or less. I've plenty to do besides watching him."

Whether or not this was Willy's real reason for avoiding his father, it was a sufficiently plausible one. All outdoor affairs at Durrus were under his control, and at any time during the morning he might be seen tramping in and out of the stable, or standing about the yard, giving orders and talking to the numerous workmen in a brogue in no way inferior to their own.

I may mention here that Willy, in common with most Irish gentlemen when speaking to the lower orders, paid them the delicate, if unintentional, compliment of temporarily adopting their accent and phraseology. I had plenty of opportunities of noticing this, as Willy evidently considered that the simplest method of providing for my amusement was to take me about with him as much as possible. I had at first rather dreaded the prospect of these constant *tête-à-têtes*, but I soon found that my cousin had always plenty to talk about, and was one of the only men I have ever met who was a good listener.

He contrived to include me in most of his comings and goings about the place. He took me down to the cove to see the seaweed carried up the rocks on donkeys' backs to be spread on the land; or I watched with deep interest while the great turf-house was slowly packed for the winter with the rough chocolate-coloured sods; or, standing at a little distance, I listened with respect to his arbitration of a dispute between two of the tenants, who generally accepted his verdict as if it had been a pronouncement of the Delphic oracle. He was very popular with the country people, as much perhaps from his invincible shrewdness as from his ready good-nature, and subsequent observation has shown me that nothing so much compels the respect and admiration of the Irish peasant as the rare astuteness that can outwit him.

Thursday was fair day at Moycullen, and

Willy, who regarded the attending of fairs as both a duty and privilege, proceeded thither with the first light of day. To say at cock-crow would scarcely be an exaggeration, for, knowing well the absurdity of expecting any servant within the walls of Durrus to call him, he had—so he informed me—resorted to the extraordinary device of putting over-night a vigorous barn-door cock on the top of his wardrobe. This bird's relentless cries at dawn were, as may be imagined, of a sufficiently rousing character, and in consequence Willy's arrival at even the most distant fairs was as a rule timely.

The result of his absence was a solitary morning for me, and lunch alone with Uncle Dominick. Although faintly alarmed at the latter prospect, I was at the same time glad of the chance which it offered of getting to know him a little better.

But in this I was disappointed. My uncle did not abate an atom of his usual impenetrable civility, and conversed with me on entirely uninteresting topics, with a fluency that was as admirable as it was provoking. I was absolutely at a loss to understand him; and, being a person sensitive to the opinions of others, I puzzled myself a great deal as to what he thought about me. The compliments which he never lost an opportunity of making, and his evident desire that Willy should do all in his power to make my visit agreeable to me, were not, I felt sure, any real indications of his feelings. That he took an interest in me, I was certain. Often I surprised in his cold eyes a still scrutiny, a watchful appraising glance that suggested mistrust, if not dislike; and although his manner was distant and self-engrossed, I had a conviction that little that I said or did escaped him.

It was a depressing day. A quiet rain trickled steadily down, and through the blurred windows the trees looked naked and disconsolate against the threatening sky. I made up my mind that it was not a day to go out, and, with a pitying thought of Willy at the fair, I heaped turf and logs upon the library fire, and determined to write a really long letter to one of my friends in America.

After a period of virtuous endeavour with this intent, I discovered that I was becoming bored to stupefaction, and gave up the struggle. There was something in the air of Durrus antagonistic to letter-writing; or perhaps it was the impossibility of writing about a place which was so different from anything that I or my correspondents had been accustomed to, and was at the same time so devoid of interest for them. I bethought me of a certain old book of field-sports which Willy had commended to my notice, and I wandered round the dusty shelves, looking for it among the exceptionally uninteresting collection of books which formed my uncle's library. Not being able to find it, I took the bold step of going to his room to ask him if he could tell me where it was.

As I went down the long dark passage that led to his room, I was keenly alive to the temerity of the proceeding, and knocked at the door with some trepidation.

" What is it ? " came an unencouraging voice from within.

" Oh ! I only wanted to ask you about a book, Uncle Dominick," I began.

The door was opened almost immediately.

" Come in, my dear Theo," said my uncle, with what was intended for a smile of welcome. " What book is it you want ? "

I explained, adding that Willy had recommended the book to me.

"Oh, Willy told you of it, did he?" said my uncle, with interest; "and you cannot find it in the library?"—turning towards a large cupboard that filled a recess on one side of the chimney-piece. "Perhaps I have it in here."

I heard a faint jingle of glass as he opened it; but the doors of fluted green silk, latticed with brass wire, prevented, from where I was standing, my seeing inside. My uncle ran his finger along one of the shelves in search of the book I wanted. Meantime I looked curiously about me.

It was a small, dingy room, disproportionately high for its size, with county and estate maps hanging on its damp-stained walls. A handsome old escritoire stood in the corner to the right of the lofty window that faced the door by which I had entered. On one or two tables, dusty pamphlets and papers lay about in a comfortless way. Right in front of the fire was a battered leather-covered armchair, in which my uncle had been sitting, though there was no book or newspaper to indicate that he had been occupied in any way.

"It is an unusual thing to hear of Willy recommending a book. I suppose this is due to your civilizing influence?" said my uncle, emerging from the recesses of the cupboard with the book in question in his hand.

"Oh, well," I replied, laughing, "this is not a very high class of literature."

"It is, nevertheless, a classic in its way," he said, opening the book; "and the prints are very good indeed."

I came and stood beside him, looking at the illustrations with him.

"The Regulator on Hertford Bridge Flat," "The Race, Epsom," "The Whissendine Brook "—we studied them together, Uncle Dominick becoming unexpectedly interesting and friendly in his reminiscences of his own sporting days when he was a young man at Oxford.

As he paused in looking at the pictures to enlarge upon an experience of his own, the pages slipped from his stiff bony fingers, and, turning over of their own accord, remained open at the title-page. There I saw, in faded ink, the words, "Owen Sarsfield, the gift of his affectionate Brother, D. S."

My uncle looked at the inscription for half an instant, and, drawing a quick breath, closed the book.

" Uncle Dominick," I said, with a sudden impulse, " won't you tell me something about my father? My mother could never bear to speak of him, and I know so little about him."

He turned his back to me, and replaced the book in the cupboard, feeling for its place in the shelves in a dull, mechanical way.

"I hate to give you pain," I went on; "but if you knew how much I have thought about him since I have been here! I have always so connected him and Durrus together in my mind."

He walked back to the fireplace, and placed one hand on the narrow marble shelf before answering.

"There are many circumstances connected with your father which make it painful for me to speak of him," he began, in a very quiet, measured voice. "I loved him very dearly; we were always together until his lamentable quarrel with my father."

He walked to the window, and stood looking out through the streaming panes, with his hands behind his back. After a few moments of waiting for him to speak again, I could bear the silence no longer.

"But what was the quarrel about? Was it my father's fault?"

"It is a hard thing to say to you," replied my uncle, turning round and looking past me into the fire, "but, under the circumstances, I feel that it is my duty to let you know the truth. Your father unfortunately got into money difficulties while at Oxford, which he was afraid to mention to his father. He went to London to study for the Bar with these debts still hanging over him, while I came home and undertook the management of the property." He paused, and passed a large silk handkerchief over his face. "Owen always had a passion for the stage; he got entangled with a theatrical set in London, and finally he took the fatal step of making himself responsible for the expenses of an —in fact, of a travelling company of actors, with, I need hardly tell you, what result. Instead of the enterprise paying his debts, as he had hoped, he found himself liable for large sums of money."

Uncle Dominick came back to the fire-place, where I was standing nervously grasping the shabby back of the leather armchair. I suppose my face told of the anxious conjectures that filled my mind, for, looking at me not unkindly, my uncle went on.

"I did all I could for him with my father, but he was a man of very violent temper, and was absolutely infuriated with Owen. He paid the debts, but he refused to see Owen again, and insisted on his leaving the country. I contrived to see him before he left England, and from that day until I got his letter saying he was ill in Cork, I neither heard of nor from him."

"But," I broke in, "why did he never write to you ?"

My uncle hesitated, and drew his hand heavily over his moustache. I saw that it trembled. He sat down in the chair by which I stood, and did not answer. I put my hand on his shoulder.

"Surely he had not quarrelled with you, Uncle Dominick ? Or was it that you—that you thought he had behaved too——" I could not finish the sentence.

"No, no, my dear," he said quickly; "I had no such feelings. I would have done anything in the world for him at that time." He cleared his throat and continued huskily, "It was Owen who misjudged me, who misconstrued all my efforts on his behalf, who ignored my offers of assistance.

I cannot bear to think of what I went through," he ended hastily, leaving his chair and again walking to the window. It was a French window, and a few stone steps led from it to the grass outside. He opened one door and looked down the drive.

It was getting darker, and the rain came driving in from the sea in ghost-like white clouds, as he stood there motionless, and apparently oblivious of the drops that fell from the roof on his head and shoulders.

" Are you looking out for Willy ? " I said at length.

" Oh, Willy ! Yes; is he not home yet ? " he answered absently, closing the window.

" Is there any portrait of my father in the house ? " I asked as he turned towards me, ignoring his remark about Willy in my anxiety to put a question that since my arrival at Durras I had often wished to ask, and feeling that it might not be easy to find another opportunity of re-opening the subject.

"There is one, taken when he was a child; it hangs in the corridor outside your bedroom door."

"But I think there are two portraits of boys there," I persisted. "I am afraid I should not know which was his."

My uncle rose wearily from his seat. "If you wish, I will show it to you now," he said. "If you will go upstairs, I will follow you in an instant."

I went slowly up the passage, and before I had reached the foot of the stairs he over-took me, and we went up together. He had his crimson silk handkerchief in his hand, and I remember wondering why he kept pressing it to his mouth as we walked along the corridor side by side.

A faint light shone through the open

door of the room over the hall door, the one that opened into mine, and against the grey light I saw in the window a crouching figure indistinctly silhouetted.

My uncle saw it too. With a muttered exclamation of anger, he walked quickly past me to the open doorway.

"What are you doing here?" he said sternly. "You know I desired you not to come upstairs, and this is the second time this week I have found you here."

He stepped back to one side, and a tall woman with a shawl covering her bent shoulders shuffled out of the room. I had already guessed that it was Moll Hourihane, and I shrank back into the doorway of my own room; but she stopped, and, stretching out her neck towards me, she fixed her eyes upon my face with an expression of hungry eagerness.

"Did you hear what I ordered you?

Go down at once," repeated my uncle, placing himself between her and me. "Let me never find you here again."

She immediately turned and slunk away round the far side of the corridor, and, looking back once more at me, disappeared through the door that led to the servants' quarters.

I gave a sigh of relief. "That woman terrifies me," I said. "I wish she would not look at me in that dreadful way."

"You need not be alarmed "—he spoke breathlessly and with unusual excitement— "she is perfectly harmless; but I do not choose to have her roaming about the house. These are the pictures of which we were speaking," he continued. "The one to the right was done of me, and this —this is the other "—pointing to an old-fashioned looking portrait of a pretty dark-haired boy holding a spaniel in his arms.

CHAPTER X.

THE MOYCULLEN HOUNDS.

" On the first day of spring, in the year '93,
  The first recreation in this countheree,
  The King's counthry gintlemen o'er hills, dales,
    and rocks,
  They rode out so gallant in search of a fox."

BLACKTHORN looked sedately amiable as Tom led him up to the hall door next morning, and I felt as I looked at him that I might safely trust him to initiate me into the mysteries of cross-country riding in the county Cork.

The day was lovely—sunny and mild, with a lingering dampness in the air that told of light rain during the night. I settled myself in the saddle, intoxicated by the idea that I was actually going out hunting for the first time, though I could not help a tremor of anxiety as I wondered if Willy would find his confidence in me had been misplaced.

I could hear him now in the hall, knocking down umbrellas and sticks in search of his whip, and presently, in response to his shouts, old Roche came shuffling to his aid.

"I was putting up your sandwiches, sir," he said.

"Go on, and give hers to Miss Theo, and hurry," said Willy's voice, in a tone indicative of exasperation.

Roche bustled out on to the steps with a small packet in his hand, a jovial smile on his face. He looked at me, and his face changed.

"My God! 'tis Master Owen himself!" he said, as if involuntarily. "I beg your pardon, miss," he continued, coming down the steps and putting the sandwiches into the saddle-pocket. "I suppose 'twas the man's hat, and the sight of you up on the horse, made me think of the young master, as we called your father."

Willy, at all times a carefully attired person, was to-day absolutely resplendent in his red coat and buckskins, and as we rode slowly down the avenue, I was impelled to tell him how smart both he and the mare looked. He beamed upon me with a simple satisfaction.

"Do you think so? Well, now, do you know what *I* was thinking? That no matter how good-looking a girl is, she always looks fifty per cent. better on a horse."

"That is a most ingenious way of praising your own horse," I said.

"Ah now, you know what I mean quite

well," rejoined Willy, with a look which was intended to be sentimental, but, by reason of his irrepressibly good spirits, rather fell away into a grin.

The meet was to be at the Clashmore cross-roads, and we passed many people on their way there. White-flannel-coated country boys and young men—" going for the best places to head the fox," as Willy observed with bitterness, and little chattering swarms of national-school children. Every now and then a young farmer or two came clattering along, on rough, short-necked horses, whose heavy tails swung from side to side as they trotted at full speed past us, and an occasional red coat gave a reality to the fact that I was going out fox-hunting. The cross-roads were now in sight, and I saw a number of riders and people who had driven to see the meet, waiting for the hounds to come up.

" Why, I declare, here are the two Miss Burkes coming along in that old shandrydan of theirs with the bedridden grey pony ! " said Willy, looking back. " Hold on, Theo. I must introduce you to them ; they're great specimens."

We allowed the pony-carriage to overtake us, and Willy, pulling off his hat with as fine a flourish as his gold hat-guard would allow, asked leave to introduce me.

" With the greatest of pleasure, Willy. Indeed, we'd no idea till yesterday, when we met Doctor Kelly in town, that Miss Sorsefield had arrived." This from the elder Miss Burke, a large, gaunt lady with a good-humoured red face and an enormous Roman nose, and a curiously deep voice, whose varying inflections ran up and down the vocal scale in booming cadences.

"You ought to be riding the pony, Miss Burke. She looks in great form."

"Oh, now, Willy! you're always joking me about poor old Zoé. You're very naughty about him. Isn't he, Bessy?"

The younger Miss Burke, thus appealed to, replied with a genteel simper, "Reely, Mimi, I'm quite ashamed of the way you and the captain go on. Don't ask me to interfere with your nonsense. We hope, Miss Sarsfield"—turning a face that was a pale dull replica of her sister's towards me—"to have the pleasure of calling upon you very soon. But oh, my gracious! there are the dogs and Mr. Dennehy coming! And look at us keeping you delaying here! Good-bye, Miss Sarsfield. I hope you'll obtain a fox."

At the cross-roads we found the master of the Moycullen hunt, a big, wild-looking man with a long reddish-grey beard and moustache, seated on an ugly yellow horse with a black stripe, like a donkey's, down his back.

"How do you do, Mr. Dennehy?" said Willy, as we rode up. "Nice day. This is my cousin, Miss Sarsfield. I hope you'll show her some sport. Morning, Nugent. How are you, Miss Connie? Do you see the new mount I have?" and Willy forgot his duties as my chaperon, in a lively conversation with Miss O'Neill.

Mr. Dennehy, with what was, I believe, unwonted condescension, began to speak to me.

"I'm delighted to see you out, Miss Sarsfield," he said in a slow, solemn brogue. "I hope we'll have a good day for you, and if there's a fox in Clashmore at all, these little hounds of mine will have him out."

I did not know much about hounds, but even to inexperienced eyes these appeared to be a very motley collection. Mr. Dennehy saw me look with interest at two strange little animals, somewhat resembling long-legged black-and-tan terriers.

" Well, Miss Sarsfield, those are the two best hounds I have, though they're ugly creatures enough. And there's a good hound. Loo, Solomon, good hound! That's a hound will only spake to game."

Here Mr. Dennehy produced a battered little horn, and with two or three bleats upon it to collect his hounds, he put the yellow horse at a yawning black ditch that divided the road from a narrow strip of rough ground, perpendicularly from which rose a steep hill covered with laurels. The yellow horse took the ditch and the low stone wall on its farther side with un-assuming skill, and he and Mr. Dennehy were presently lost to sight in the wood.

Willy now came up to me with Miss

O'Neill and her brother, and I was introduced to the former, a small, fair-haired girl in a smart habit, with brown eyes and rather a high colour. She nodded to me with cheery indifference, and continued her conversation with Willy, leaving me to talk to her brother.

This I found to be a somewhat difficult task. His manner was exceedingly polite, but he appeared to be engrossed in watching the covert, and we finally relapsed into silence. At intervals Mr. Dennehy's red coat showed between the low close-growing trees as he led his horse through the covert, and we could hear his original method of encouraging his hounds.

"Thatsy me darlins! Thatsy-atsy-atsy! Turrn him out, Woodbine! Hi, Waurior, good hound!"

I felt inclined to laugh, but as no one else seemed amused, I refrained and waited for further developments. Presently, with a few words to Willy, Mr. O'Neill put spurs to his big bay and galloped off. In a moment or two, Miss O'Neill, without further ceremony, followed her brother to the other end of the covert, and Willy and I remained with about twenty other riders on the road.

"See here!" he said in low, excited tones. "You keep close to me. Old Dennehy's got a beastly trick of slipping away with his hounds directly they find, and making fools of the whole field, leaving them the wrong side of the covert. But I think we're in a good place here. Whisht! wasn't that a hound speaking? Come on this way."

We set off down the road helter-skelter after Mr. O'Neill and Connie, but were stopped by an excited rush of country boys with shouts of, "He's gone aisht! He's broke the far side!" and at the same instant Mr. and Miss O'Neill came pounding down a ride out of the covert.

"It's just as I thought; Dennehy's gone away with the hounds by himself," called out Mr. O'Neill. "A country fellow saw the fox heading for Lick, and Dennehy all alone with the hounds, going like mad!"

At this juncture I think it better not to record Willy's remarks.

"It's all right, Nugent," said Connie. "I know a way over the hill lower down."

"Don't mind her, Theo," said Willy in my ear; "just you stick to me."

We had galloped past the eastern bound of the wood, and as he spoke he turned his horse and jumped the fence on the right of the road. Blackthorn followed of his own accord, and I found that an Irish bank did not feel as difficult as it looked.

Willy turned in his saddle to watch me.

"Well done! that's your sort," he shouted. "Hold him now, and hit him! This is a big place we're coming to."

We were over before I had time to think, and to my horror I saw that Willy was making for a hill that looked like the side of a house, covered with furze.

"There's a way up here, but you'll have to lead. Nip off! I'll go first."

I was fearfully out of breath, but Willy allowed no time for delay. Up the hill we scrambled, Blackthorn leading me considerably more than I led him. After the first few seconds of climbing, I felt as if it would be impossible to go on. My habit hindered me at every step. Blackthorn's jerks and tugs at the reins nearly threw me on my face, and the fear of Willy alone prevented me from letting him finish the ascent by himself. When at last we reached the top, Willy and I were both so much out of breath that we could not speak, and I wished for nothing so much as to lie down. But Willy, with a blazing face, made signs to me to mount at once, and, jerking me into the saddle, we again set off.

The top of the hill which we had now gained was rough, boggy ground. Down to our right lay the gleaming laurel covert, and in front of us the hill sloped gradually down into a low tract of bog and lakes, with hills beyond. We could see nothing of any one, but a countryman, on the top of a bank above the wood, waved semaphore-like directions that the hounds were running to the north-east.

"Hullo! here's Nugent," said Willy, in a not over-pleased voice, and as he spoke I saw Mr. O'Neill's bay horse coming along over the hill. He soon overtook us, looking, I was glad to see, as heated and dishevelled as Willy and I.

"I knew that way of Connie's was no use, so I came back and went up the hill after you. Where are the hounds?"

"Going north-east, a fellow told me. But look! By Jove! there they are on the hill across the bog, and going straight for Killnavoodhee."

"There is only one way to pick them up," said Nugent, with what seemed to me unnatural calm—"we must cross the bog."

"But, my dear fellow, I don't believe there's a way across, and once we got in, we'd not get out in a hurry."

"Do you mind trying, Miss Sarsfield?' demanded Mr. O'Neill.

"Whatever Willy likes," I said.

"Oh, all right," said Willy. "Fire away, but you'll have to pay for the funeral, Nugent."

We had now reached the foot of the hill, and we rode rapidly along the verge of the bog for a short distance till we came to where an old fence traversed it in a north-easterly direction.

" Here's the place. If we can get along the top of this, we shall just hit off their line," Mr. O'Neill said. He went first, and the horses picked their way along the top of the bank like cats, though the sides crumbled under their feet, and sometimes the whole structure tottered as if it were going to collapse into the deep dykes on either side. At last it broke sharp off, at a pool of black mire. Our guide dismounted and jumped down into the bog, pulling his horse after him, and we slowly dragged our way through the heavy ground to the farther side of the bog.

Here we were confronted by the most formidable obstacle we had yet come to. It consisted of a low, soft-looking bank, with an immense boggy ditch beyond it.

"We've got to try it, I suppose," said Willy, "but it's a thundering big jump, and there's a deuced bad landing beyond the water."

He and Mr. O'Neill remounted, and the former put his horse at the place. The bay's hoofs sank deep in the bank, but he took a spring that landed him safely on the opposite side on comparatively firm ground. My turn came next.

"Whip him over it!" exclaimed Willy.

I did so as well as I was able, but the treacherous ground broke under Blackthorn's feet, and he all but floundered back into the ditch as he landed.

"Oh, Willy!" I cried, "I'm afraid you'll never get her over now that the bank is broken."

But Willy was already too much occupied with Alaska to make any reply. She refused several times, but finally, yielding to the inevitable, she threw herself rather than jumped off the bank, and the next moment she and Willy were in the ditch.

I was terrified as to the consequences, and was much relieved when I saw Willy, black from head to foot, crawl from the mare's back on to the more solid mud of the bank on our side. Without a word he caught Alaska by the head, and began to try and pull her out. His extraordinary appearance, and the fact that he was much too angry to be in the least conscious of its absurdity, had the disastrous effect of reducing both Mr. O'Neill and me to helpless laughter.

"I am very sorry, Willy," I panted, "and I am delighted you're not hurt; but if you could only see yourself!"

Willy silently continued his efforts.

"Oh, Mr. O'Neill, do get down and help him," I continued.

"I don't want any help, thank you," returned my cousin, with restrained fury. "Come up out of that, you brute!"—applying his hunting-crop with vigour to the recumbent Alaska, who thereupon, with two or three violent efforts, heaved herself out of the slough. All this time Mr. O'Neill had been grinning with that unfeigned delight which all hunting-men seem to derive from the misfortunes of their friends.

"You have toned down that new coat, Willy," he remarked; "and I must say the little mare takes to water like an otter."

"Oh, I dare say it's very funny indeed!" retorted Willy, leading Alaska on to the higher ground where we were standing; "but if you'd an eye in your head you'd see the mare is dead lame."

"By George! so she is. That's hard

luck. She must have given herself a strain."

"Well, whatever ails her, there's no use in your standing there looking at me," replied Willy. "I can get home all right. I don't want Theo to lose the run, and you'll head them yet if you put on the pace."

His magnanimity was almost more crushing than his wrath. I was filled with contrition for my heartless amusement, and begged to be allowed to stay with him. But I was given no voice in the matter; my offer was scouted, and before I had fairly grasped the situation, I was galloping up a narrow mountain road after Nugent O'Neill.

CHAPTER XI.

NUGENT O'NEILL.

"He is the toniest aristocrat on the boat."

AFTER we had gone about a quarter of a mile, my companion pulled up.

"I think our best chance is to wait here," he said. "From the way the hounds were running, they are almost certain to come this way eventually."

The road up which we had ridden formed the only pass between the hills on either side of us, and beyond was a low-lying level stretch of country.

"If he'll only run down that way——"

Mr. O'Neill began, but suddenly stopped, and silently pointed with his whip to the hill at our right.

"What is it?" I asked, in incautiously loud tones.

He looked for an instant as if he were going to shake his whip at me, and again pointed, this time to a narrow strip of field beside the road. I saw what looked like a little brown shadow fleeting across it, and in another moment the fox appeared on the top of the wall a few yards ahead of us. He looked about him as if considering his next move, and then, seeing us, he leaped into the road and, running along it, vanished over the crest of the hill.

Mr. O'Neill turned to me with such excitement that he seemed a different person. "Here are the hounds!" he said, "and not a soul with them."

Down the hill the pack came like a

torrent, and were over the wall in a second. They spread themselves over the road in front of us as if at fault; but one of the little black-and-tan hounds justified Mr. Dennehy's good opinion by picking up the line, and at once the whole pack were racing full cry up the road.

I have often looked back with considerable amusement to that moment. I was suddenly possessed by a kind of frenzy of excitement that deprived me of all power of speech. I heard my companion tell me to keep as close to him as I could, but I was incapable of any response save an inebriated smile and a wholly absurd flourish of my whip.

As this does not purport to be a hunting-story, I will not describe the run which followed. I believe it lasted fifteen minutes, and included some of the traditional "big leps" of the country. But to me it was merely an indefinite period of delirious happiness. I scarcely felt Blackthorn jump, and was only conscious of the thud of the big bay horse's hoofs in front of me and the rushing of the wind in my ears. At last a wood seemed to heave up before me; the bay horse was pulled up sharply, and I found myself almost in the middle of the hounds.

" By George ! he's just saved his brush," said Mr. O'Neill, breathlessly ; " he's gone to ground in there, and I am afraid we shall never get him out. I hope you are none the worse for your gallop," he continued politely. " It was pretty fast while it lasted." He dismounted as he spoke, and began to investigate the hole in which the fox had taken refuge, and while he was thus engaged I saw Mr. Dennehy on his yellow horse coming across the next field. When he came up he was, rather to my surprise, amiably pleased at our success in picking up the hounds, and regretted we had not killed our fox.

"You two and meself were the only ones in this run," he said.

My thoughts at once reverted to poor Willy. I asked Mr. Dennehy if he had seen anything of him, and heard that he had passed my cousin, slowly making his way home.

"Oh, I think I ought to go home at once," I said to Mr. O'Neill. "I might overtake him if you will tell me where I am to go."

"If you will allow me, I think you had better let me show you the way," he answered, with a resumption of the stiff manner which had at first struck me. Although I was quite aware that politeness alone prompted this offer, my ignorance of the country made it impossible for me to refuse it. Trusting, however, that by speedily overtaking Willy I should be able to release my unwilling pilot, I wished Mr. Dennehy good morning, and we made the best of our way to the nearest road.

Our way lay through what seemed to me a chessboard of absurdly small fields. I could not imagine where all the stones came from that were squandered in the heaping up of the walls that divided them from each other, nor did I greatly care, so long as the necessity of jumping them gave me something to amuse me, and made conversation with Mr. O'Neill disjointed and unexacting.

What little I had seen of him at the covert-side had not inspired me with any anxiety to pursue his acquaintance, and once we had got out on to the road, with all the responsibilities of a *tête-à-tête* staring us in the face, my heart died within me.

Never had I met any one who was so difficult to talk to. I found that I was gradually assuming the ungrateful position of a catechist, and, while filled with smothered indignation at my companion's perfunctory answers, I could not repress a certain admiration for the composure with which he allowed the whole stress of discourse to rest upon my shoulders. I at length made up my mind to give myself no more trouble in the cause of politeness, and resolved that until he chose to speak I would not do so.

A long silence was the result. We rode on side by side, my companion staring steadily between his horse's ears, while I wondered how soon we should be likely to meet Willy, and thought how very much more I should have preferred his society.

"I suppose you find this place rather

dull?" Mr. O'Neill's uninterested voice at last broke the silence. "I have always heard that American young ladies had a very gay time."

I at once felt that this insufferable young man was trying to talk down to my level —the level of an "American young lady"—and my smouldering resentment got the better of my politeness.

"I very seldom find myself bored by places. It is, as a rule, the people of the place that bore me."

"Really," he returned, with perfect serenity. "Yes, I dare say that is true; but ladies do not generally get on very well without shop and dances."

"Strange as it may appear, neither of those entrancing occupations are essential to my happiness."

Mr. O'Neill turned and looked at me with faint surprise, but made no reply.

Another pause ensued, and I began to repent of my crossness.

It was clearly my turn to make the next remark, and I said, in a more conciliatory voice—

"I suppose you don't have very much to do here, either?"

"Oh, I am not here very much, and I can always get as much shooting and fishing as I want; but I fancy my sisters find it rather dull."

"Are your sisters fond of music? I was very glad to find a piano at Durrus."

His face assumed for the first time a look of interest.

"My elder sister plays a good deal; and Connie has a banjo, though I cannot say she knows much about it; and I play the fiddle a little. I believe in these parts we are considered quite a gifted family."

I felt that I had, so to speak, "struck ile."

"Do you play the violin?" I said, with excitement. "I delight in playing accompaniments! I hope you will bring your music with you when you come to dinner."

"Oh, thanks very much; my sister always accompanies me," he responded coolly.

His deliberate self-possession was infinitely exasperating in my then state of mind, and I repented the enthusiasm that had laid me open to this snub. I was hurriedly framing an effective rejoinder, when he again spoke, this time in tones of considerable amusement.

"Do you see that man leading a lame horse down the road? If he is not a chimney-sweep, I think he must be your cousin."

As we came nearer, I was secretly unspeakably tickled by Willy's inky and bedraggled appearance; but I was too proud to join in Mr. O'Neill's open amusement, until I noticed for the first time the incongruously rakish effect imparted to Willy's forlorn figure by the fact that his hat had been crushed in. My injured dignity collapsed, and, holding on to my saddle for support, I laughed till the tears poured down my cheeks.

It was at this singularly unpropitious moment that Willy, hearing our horses' feet, turned round.

"Oh, there you are!" he called out. "Did you meet the hounds?" Then, in a voice which showed his good temper had not returned. "You seem to be greatly amused, whatever you did."

I thought it better to ignore the latter part of the sentence, and dashed at once into a confused account of our exploits, Mr. O'Neill helping out my narrative with a few geographical details; to all of which Willy listened with morose attention.

" And Blackthorn jumped splendidly. Willy," I said. " I was so sorry you weren't there."

" H'm!" said Willy; " very kind of you, I'm sure."

Mr. O'Neill saw that the situation was becoming strained.

" As I can't be of any further help to you or Miss Sarsfield," he said, " I think I will go back and look for the hounds;" and, wishing us good-bye, he rode off.

" Well," Willy began viciously, " you seem to find O'Neill cheerful enough, after all."

" *Indeed*, I don't, Willy," I said, with vigour; " he was perfectly *odious*."

" You didn't look as if you thought him so a while ago, when you were both near falling off your horses with laughing. I suppose "—with sudden penetration—" that it was at me you were laughing."

" Oh no, Willy; at least, it was not exactly you—indeed, it was only your hat."

Even at this supreme moment the air of disreputable gaiety of Willy's headgear was too much for me, and my voice broke into a hysterical shriek. This was the last straw. With a wrathful glance, he turned his back upon me, and stalked silently on beside Alaska. Blackthorn and I followed meekly in the rear, and in this order we soberly proceeded to Durrus.

CHAPTER XII.

A VOYAGE OF DISCOVERY.

" And wouldst thou leave me thus? Say Nay."

A LOWERING grey sky succeeded the sunshine of the day of the hunt. I crawled down late to breakfast, feeling very stiff after yesterday's exertions, and was on the whole relieved to find that Willy had gone out for a long day's shooting, and that till lunch at least I should have no one to entertain but myself.

The evening before had been, as far as Willy had been concerned, of a rather complicated type. I had done all in my power to efface from his mind the memory of my unfortunate laughter, but until dinner was over he had remained implacable. Uncle Dominick, on the contrary, had been unusually bland and talkative. It appeared that Madam O'Neill and her eldest daughter had called on me while I was out, and my uncle, having met them on the drive, had brought them in, given them tea, and had even gone so far as to ask the two girls to come with their brother to dinner the next night. He had given me to understand that this unusual hospitality was on my account—"Although," he added, " I have no doubt you two young people are quite well able to amuse each other." The look which accompanied this was, under the circumstances, so peculiarly embarrassing, that, in order to change the conversation, I made the mistake of beginning to describe the hunt. Too soon I discovered that to slur over Willy's disaster would be impossible, and my obvious efforts to do so did not improve matters.

"So you went off with young O'Neill," my uncle had said, with a change of look and voice that frightened me ; and nothing more was said on the subject.

My discomfiture was perhaps the cause of the alteration in Willy's demeanour after dinner. Success far beyond my expectations, or indeed my wishes, was the result of my conciliatory advances. I went to bed feeling that I had more than regained the position I had held in Willy's esteem, and a little flurried by the difficulties of so ambiguous a relationship as that of first cousins.

From all this, it may be imagined that when I heard from Roche that "the masther was gone to town, and would not be home for lunch," I regarded the combined absences of Willy and his father as little short of providential.

I observed that the magenta and yellow dahlias which had decorated the table on my arrival still held their ground, albeit in an advanced stage of decay; and, remembering the glories of the autumn leaves, I suggested to Roche that with his permission I might be able to improve upon the present arrangement.

A little elated by the expectation of surprising Willy with the unusual splendour of the dinner-table, and not without an emulative thought of the O'Neills, I determined to ransack the shrubberies for the most glowing leaves wherewith to carry out my purpose. A few minutes later, I left the house with a capacious basket in my hand, feeling a delightful sense of freedom, and full of the selfish, half-savage pleasure of a solitary and irresponsible voyage of discovery.

I wandered down the nearest path to the sea, and, keeping to the shore, came to the little promontory which, with its few ragged trees, I could see from the windows of my room. There was a certain romance about this lonely wind and wave beaten point that had always attracted me to it. When, in the early light, I saw the fir trees' weird reflection in the quiet cove, I used to wonder if they had ever been a landmark for some western Dick Hatteraick; and now, as I scrambled about, and tugged at the tough bramble-stems that trailed in the coarse grass, I was half persuaded that any one of the rough boulders might close the entrance of a smuggler's long-forgotten " hide."

I had soon gathered as many blackberry-leaves as I wanted, and, sitting down beside one of the old trees, I leaned my cheek against its seamy trunk and looked across the grey rollers to the horizon.

A narrow black line stole from behind the eastern point of Durrusmore Harbour, leaving a dark stain on the sky as it went, and from where I sat I fancied I could hear the beat of machinery.

It was the first time I had noticed the passing of one of the big American steamers, and I watched the great creature move out of sight with a strange conflict of feeling. Uppermost, I think, was the thought of what my regret would be if I were at that moment on board her, bound for America. I was a little ashamed when I reflected how soon the newer interests had superseded the old. I had been but a week in Ireland, and already the idea of leaving it for America was akin to that of emigration. What, I wondered, was the charm that had worked so quickly? Was this subtle familiarity and satisfaction with my new life merely the result of æsthetic interest, or had it the depth of an inherited instinct?

I could not tell; I could only feel a strange presentiment that my existence had hitherto been nothing but a preface, and that I was now on the threshold of what was to be, for good or evil, my real life.

I picked up my basket and retraced my steps down the little slope, till I again found myself in the shrubbery walk. On one point my mind was clear. My liking for Durrus was in no perceptible degree influenced by my feeling for my uncle and my cousin. I reiterated this to myself as I strolled along in the damp shade of over-arching laurels towards the plantation which lay between the sea and the lodge.

Uncle Dominick was anything but a

person to inspire immediate affection; and then Willy—well, Willy certainly had many attractive points, but, although he was a pleasant companion, he could not be said to be either very cultured or refined.

I left the path and strayed through the wood, stopping here and there to rob the branches of their lavish autumn loveliness. A sluggish little stream crept among the trees, and along its banks the ferns grew thickly. I knelt down in the stubbly yellow grass beside it, where the pale trunk of a beech tree stooped over the water, and picked the small delicate ferns that were clustering between its roots. Having gathered all within reach, I still knelt there, watching a little procession of withered beech-leaves making their slow way down the stream, and studying my own dark reflection on the water.

I was at length startled by the sound of

voices that seemed to come from the path I had just left, but from where I was, the thickness of the intervening laurels prevented me from seeing to whom they belonged.

It soon became evident that one of the speakers was a country girl. She was talking rapidly and earnestly; but what she said was unintelligible to me till she and her companion came to the point in the path which was nearest to me, when, after a momentary pause, the soft voice broke out—

" Ye won't lave me for her, will ye, now ? Ye *said* ye'd hold by me always, and now—— "

Something between a sob and a choke ended the sentence. Several sobs followed; and then the girl's voice went on excitedly—

" Ah ! 'tis no use your goin' on like that;

ye know ye want to have done with me entirely."

I could hear no reply; but that re-assurance and consolation were offered was obvious, for as the footsteps died away I heard something like a broken laugh from the girl, with some faint echo of it from a man's voice.

"Who can she be?" I thought, with instinctive compassion. There was a certain perplexing familiarity in the low pathetic voice, and I walked home, feeling unnecessarily depressed and troubled by what I had heard, and wondering sadly at the self-abandonment which had led to such an appeal.

The path by which I returned skirted the garden and formed a loop with the one by which I had first entered the wood. As I approached the broader walk, I saw a girl's figure flit down the other path, and I had just time to recognize it as being that of Anstey Brian. Simultaneously came the recollection of the pleading voice in the wood, and in an instant I knew why it had been familiar.

"Then it must have been Anstey," I thought, feeling both sorry and surprised. The entreaty in her voice had made it very plain how serious a matter her trouble was to her, and the helplessness of her quick surrender showed that she had lost all power of resistance or resentment. I was astonished to think that so pretty a girl as Anstey should have cause to reproach her sweetheart with want of constancy. "Who could he be?" I wondered. Then, remembering that the path she was on was a usual short cut from the lodge to the yard, I came to the conclusion that one of the Durrus stablemen must have been the object of this broken-hearted appeal.

I determined that I would try and find out something further about Anstey and her lover, and wondered if it would be of any use to mention the subject to Willy.

CHAPTER XIII.

A DINNER-PARTY.

" Go, let him have a table by himself !
For he does neither affect company,
Nor is he fit for't, indeed."

In spite of the incontestable success of my decorations, which drew forth the admiration of even the superior Henrietta O'Neill, I felt, before we had arrived at the period of fish, that the dinner-party was likely to be a failure.

Uncle Dominick had, of course, taken in the elder Miss O'Neill, and as far as they were concerned nothing was left to be desired. Conversation of a fluent and high-class order was evidently her strong point. She at once entered upon a discussion of Irish politics with my uncle in a manner deserving of all praise, and as I surreptitiously studied her pale, plain, intellectual face, with the dark hair severely drawn back, and heard her enunciate her opinions in clearly framed sentences, I became deeply conscious of my own general inferiority.

Nevertheless, I did what in me lay to talk to Nugent O'Neill, who had taken me in, thus leaving to Willy the necessary and, as I thought, congenial task of entertaining Miss Connie. Nothing could apparently be better arranged. Nugent had exchanged his frigid, uninterested civility of the day before for an excellent semblance of sociability, beneath which, as it seemed to me, he concealed a curious observation of all that I said. He had a dark clever face, with strong well-cut features, and blue eyes, with a pleasanter expression in them than I had at first expected to see there. His voice would have been monotonous in its quietness and unexcitability had it not been for a certain humorous, semi-American turn which he occasionally imparted to his sentences. He annoyed me, but at the same time he was interesting; moreover—which was to me a very strong point in his favour—he was evidently as much alive as I to the fact that for the next hour and a half it would be our solemn duty to amuse each other, and to that intent we both performed prodigies of agreeability.

But Willy was the cause of disaster. I became gradually aware that silence was settling down upon him and Connie, and that, instead of devoting himself to her, he, with his eyes fixed on me and my partner, was listening moodily to what we were saying. When this had gone on for some minutes, during which Connie crumbled her bread and looked cross, I was exasperated to the point of bestowing a glance upon him calculated to awaken in him a sense of his bad manners. Far, however, from accepting my reproof, Willy returned my look with a gaze of admiring defiance, and projected himself into our conversation by flatly contradicting what Nugent was saying. The latter rose many degrees in my estimation by ignoring the interruption till he had reached the end of his sentence. Then, with a tolerating smile, he looked past me to Willy, and asked him what he had said.

Willy's dark eyebrows met in a way that unpleasantly reminded me of his father.

" If it wasn't worth listening to, it's not worth repeating," he said aggressively.

Terrified by the turn things were taking, I struck in quickly, " Oh, Willy! have you told Miss O'Neill what you heard to-day about the Jackson-Crolys giving a ball ? "

" No; I thought she'd have heard it herself," he returned ungraciously.

" As it happens, I had heard nothing about it," said Connie, from the other side of the table; " but I cannot say that I feel much excited at the prospect of one of their dances."

" I am looking forward to it immensely," I said, persevering with my topic. " I want very much to see a real Irish ball."

" Yes," said Nugent, reflectively; " you will see that to great perfection at the Jackson-Crolys'. They excel in old Irish hospitality. They do that kind of thing in quite the traditional way. Little Croly offers you whiskey the moment you get into the hall; and, though you may not believe it, Mrs. Jackson-Croly orders champagne to be put into all the carriages when people are coming away. The guests are generally pretty happy by that time, and she says it is to keep their hearts up on the way home."

"That's quite true," observed Connie; "and, as well as I remember, you were not at all above drinking it next day."

"Do they dance jigs at these entertainments?" I asked. "If so, I am afraid I shall be rather out of it."

"Oh yes," said Willy, with what was intended to be biting sarcasm; "and hornpipes and Highland flings. They always do at Irish dances."

"Nonsense, Willy! They don't really, do they, Mr. O'Neill?"

"It is always well to be prepared for emergencies," he answered, "so I should advise you to have some lessons from Willy. I have been told that step-dancing is his strongest suit."

" Who told you that ? " demanded Willy.

" One of our men was at McCarthy's wedding the other day, and said he saw you there."

" Oh yes," supplemented Connie. " He said, 'The sight would lave your eyes to see Mr. Sarsfield and that little gerr'l of owld Michael Brian's taking the flure, and they so souple and so springy.' "

Willy did not appear to be at all amused by this flattering opinion, or by the admirable accent in which it was repeated. On the contrary, he looked rather disconcerted, and, with a glance towards the other end of the table, he said awkwardly—

" Oh, one has to do these sort of things now and then. The people like it, and it doesn't do me any harm."

"On the contrary," said Nugent, "I am sure it is a most healthy exercise. But I thought it rather spoiled your leg for a top-boot."

Willy was known to favour knee-breeches as being especially becoming to him, and at this, to my great relief, he turned his back upon us, and plunged into an ostentatiously engrossing conversation with Connie. At last we were in smooth water, and with almost a sigh of relief I heard Nugent take up the thread of our discourse at the point where Willy had broken it off.

It was evident that he could be pleasant enough when he chose; and though I felt that this new development was almost as offensive in another way as his deliberate dullness yesterday, I was now very grateful for its timely help. At the same time, I bore in mind with resentment my unremunerated toil during our ride, and reflected bitterly on the fact that people who only talk when it pleases them, receive far more credit when they do so than those who from a sense of duty exhaust themselves conversationally.

Uncle Dominick and Henrietta had up to this not caused me a moment's anxiety. We were now at dessert, and yet the flow of their discourse had never flagged. In fact, my uncle seemed at present to be delivering a species of harangue, to which Henrietta was attending with a polite unconvinced smile. This was all as it should be, and my respect for Henrietta's social gifts increased tenfold. Unfortunately, however, it soon became evident that the discussion, whatever it was, was taking rather too personal a tone, and my uncle's voice became so loud and overbearing that Nugent and I were constrained to listen to him.

"You amaze me," he was saying. "I cannot believe that any sane person can honestly hold such absurd theories. What! do you mean to tell me that one of my tenants, a creature whose forefathers have lived for centuries in ignorance and degradation, is my equal?"

"His degradation is merely the result of injustice," said Miss O'Neill, coolly adjusting her *pince-nez*.

"I deny it," said my uncle, loudly. His usually pale face was flushed, and his eyes burned. "But that is not the point. What I maintain is that any fusion of classes such as you advocate, would have the effect of debarring the upper while it entirely failed to raise the lower orders. If you were to marry your coachman, as, according to your theories of equality, I suppose you would not hesitate to do, do you think these latent instincts of refinement that you talk about would make him a fit companion for you and your family? You know as well as I do that such an idea is preposterous. It is absurd to suppose that the natural arrangement of things can be tampered with. This is a subject on which I feel very strongly, and it shocks me to hear a young lady in your position advance such opinions!"

Henrietta's face assumed an aggravating expression, clearly conveying her opinion that further argument would be thrown away. Uncle Dominick gulped down a glass of wine, and glared round the table. There was a general silence, and I took advantage of it to make a move to the drawing-room.

I was wholly taken aback by my uncle's violence, and could not help fearing that the number of times his glass had been replenished had had something to say to it.

Willy's temper had also been so uncertain that I dreaded an outbreak between him and his father, and, in the interval of waiting for their reappearance, I found myself making the most absent and ill-chosen answers to Henrietta's questions upon the culture and political status of American women, while I listened anxiously for the sound of the opening of the dining-room door. My only consolation was, that Nugent would, for his own sake, do his best to keep the peace, and I was surprised to find how much I relied on his powers of doing so.

In my preoccupied state of mind, it is not to be wondered at that Henrietta soon appeared to come to the conclusion that I was incapable of giving her any information on the subjects in which she was interested, and that I was generally a person of limited abilities. She leaned back in her chair with the exhausted air of one who relinquishes a hopeless task, and, taking up a photograph-book, she tacitly made me over to her sister.

Connie's ideas ran in less exalted grooves. The run of the day before was to her a topic of inexhaustible interest ; and when she found that my humility in the matter of hunting equalled my ignorance, she expanded into extreme graciousness, and was soon in the full tide of narration. The story-teller who treats of hunting with any real enthusiasm generally loses all mental perspective, and sacrifices artistic unity to historical accuracy. Then, as now, I was amazed at the powers of memory and merciless fidelity to detail with which those who have taken part in a run can afterwards describe it, and I listened with reverence befitting the neophyte to Connie's adventures by flood and field.

Foxes and fences, hounds and hunters, were revolving in my brain, when the opening of the door brought the story to a conclusion, and Willy came into the room, followed by Nugent. He marched directly to the sofa where I was sitting, and deposited himself beside me with such determination that the rebound of its springs almost lifted me into the air.

This behaviour was really intolerable. Willy had not before shown any very pronounced partiality for me, and why he should have selected this evening for a demonstration of affection it would be hard to say. One thing was clear: it must be suppressed with a strong hand, or a deadlock would ensue. Nugent was standing on the hearthrug, with apparently no prospect of entertainment before him save what he could derive from talking to his sisters; while those two young ladies were well aware that no reasonable hostess could ask them to dinner and expect them to devote their evening to conversing with their brother, and, pending action on my part, were sitting in expectant silence. I turned upon Willy in desperation.

"You *must* talk to them," I hissed in his ear.

To which, with equal emphasis, he whispered back, "I won't!" fixing upon me a blandly stubborn gaze that infuriated me beyond the bounds of endurance.

I leaped from my seat, and, with a timely recollection of Nugent's violin, I walked over to him and asked if he had remembered to bring it. He admitted apologetically that it was in the hall, adding, with unexpected modesty, that he had only brought it because I had asked him to do so. I had some acquaintance with the ways of amateur violinists, and speedily recognized the diffidence which conceals a yearning to play at all hazards. My intention to dislike him was softened by the discovery that he was not at all points so superior as I had believed, and I was pleased to notice some hurry and trepidation in his manner while he was tuning his violin. Henrietta advanced upon the piano with an air of sisterly resignation, and, concealing a yawn, tapped a note for Nugent to tune by.

While he was thus engaged, I cast an anxious eye round the room. My uncle had now come in, and, with his elbow on the chimney-piece, was looking into the fire. Connie had taken possession of the ancient photograph-book which her sister had put down, and, in company with Willy, was silently and methodically turning over its yellow pages. Well did I know its contents. Ladies in preposterously inflated skirts, with rows of black velvet round the tail; and gentlemen clad from head to heel in decent black, each with his back to an Italian landscape, and his tall hat on a Grecian pedestal near him—all alike undistinguishable and unknown. I felt sincerely for Connie; but other occupation there was none, and I had done my best on her behalf.

I was at first inclined to agree with Nugent in his own estimate of his playing, and I saw with unworthy amusement that he was extremely nervous; but as he went on he steadied down, and played with considerable sweetness and delicacy. The keen notes vibrated in the dim, lofty room, and tingling in the many hanging crystals of the old glass chandelier. I forgot the indignation which he had yesterday aroused in me, and remained leaning on the piano, conscious only of the pleasure I was receiving, until the player ceased, and began to unscrew his bow preparatory to putting it away.

"Please play something else," I said hastily. "Won't you try this Suite of Corelli's? I know it so well."

"I am afraid my sister doesn't know the accompaniment," he answered, with a dubious look at Henrietta, who was rising from the piano.

Her bored manner had already told me that she looked on accompanying her brother as a task beneath her powers, and the thought struck me with paralyzing conviction that I ought to have asked her to play a solo. However, this was not the moment to rectify the error; Nugent was lingering over the putting away of his violin, with an obvious desire to play again.

"I suppose it would be too much to

ask you to try it?" he said to me, after another glance at Henrietta's unresponsive face.

"Perhaps if it was not very difficult I might be able——" I said, and checked myself, remembering the snub I had received on that very subject.

But now that I had admitted so much, Nugent held me to my word, and firmly proceeded to arrange the piano part on the desk for me.

"I don't envy you, Miss Sarsfield," remarked Henrietta, with a cold little laugh; "Nugent's ideas of counting are excessively primitive."

Decidedly Henrietta was annoyed.

"I am the class of savage who cannot count more than five," he replied, addressing me; "but I do my best."

Miss O'Neill laughed again. "You will have to play it for him," she said, moving away from the piano; "Nugent is a regular bully."

I scarcely liked being coerced in this way, but I yielded; and we played the piece I had asked for, as well as several others, before I remembered my duties as hostess. Willy had forsaken Connie and the photograph-book, and had again left her and Henrietta to talk to each other, while he propped himself against the chimney-piece, and gazed moodily at Nugent and me.

I could not have believed that he would have left me in this dastardly way to bear the burden and heat of the entertainment, and I made a second effort to keep things going by begging Miss O'Neill to play. But this time I was unsuccessful; she would not be propitiated. A look passed between her and her sister, whose banjo I now had little doubt had been secreted in

the hall; while I, in violation of all the
laws of civility, had myself been monopo-
lizing the piano. They both got up from
their places.

"I should have been delighted," said
Henrietta, "but I am afraid it is getting
rather late. My dear Nugent"—calling to
her brother, who was carefully swaddling
his violin preparatory to putting it away—
"we really ought to be getting home.
The carriage must have been waiting some
time; and I am sure"—in a lower voice—
"that Mr. Sarsfield has had quite enough
of us."

I looked at my uncle, who during the
violin-playing had sunk into an armchair,
and had shaded his eyes with his hand, as
if listening attentively. He had not
moved since we stopped, and looked almost
as if he were asleep; but there was something in his attitude that conveyed the

idea of deep dejection rather than of slumber.

The general stir of departure roused him. He rose slowly, and said good night with a little more than his usual sombreness.

CHAPTER XIV.

IN SOCIETY.

" Ah ! Then was it all spring weather?
  Nay, but we were young and together."

" Society is now one polished horde
  Formed of two mighty tribes, the Bores and Bored."

ONE day at Durrus was very like another.
By the time I had been there three weeks
or a month, the days stretched out behind
me into indefinite length, separating me
more and more from my past life.

Looking back to that time, it seems to
resolve itself into one long *tête-à-tête* with
Willy. Quiet rides with him through the
damp brown woods, or now and then a
day with the Moycullen hounds ; drives

to return the visits of such of the natives as had called upon me; walks across the turf bog to where the old graveyard hangs over the sea, to watch the sun drop below the horizon. "Bound for America," says Willy. "I wonder if you'd like to be going back with him?" I had no doubts in my own mind on the subject, though I did not feel called upon to say so to him. I was now quite certain that, in spite of various drawbacks, I enjoyed my life at Durrus very much.

I have said that I had had callers. After the O'Neills, among the first to come and see me were Mrs. Jackson-Croly and her daughters, and the Burkes, whose acquaintance I had already made.

These ladies all made their appearance on the same afternoon; but before the Burkes arrived I had an undiluted quarter of an hour of the Jackson-Crolys, during which time the magnificence of Mrs. Croly's manner was only equalled by the fashionable languor of her daughters'. I naturally tried to talk to them of such local subjects as I knew anything about, but found that the meanest topic on which they would consent to converse was Dublin Castle, and the affability displayed to them by the lord-lieutenant—" left'nant," they pronounced it—during the past season. With these lofty themes I was quite unfitted to grapple, and had sunk into a subordinate place in the conversation when the Miss Burkes were announced.

They were both exceedingly cordial and friendly, and Miss Mimi began almost immediately to rally me with ponderous facetiousness on my exploits on the day of the hunt.

" Oh, Miss Sarsfield ! what's this we hear about you and Mr. O'Neill ? Springing away through the country after the fox, and leaving poor Willy in the ditch! Oh, fie!"

I feel that it is hopeless to convey any adequate idea of Miss Mimi's voice by any system of spelling; but the fact that in her vocabulary "fie," was pronounced "foy," may serve as some indication of her manner of speech.

At her ingenuous observation I became aware that the eyes of Mrs. Jackson-Croly and her two daughters were riveted upon me with undisguised interest, and I hastened to explain how it was that Willy had been left behind. But Miss Burke paid little heed; another and more exciting topic had suggested itself to her.

"Well, Mrs. Croly, is it true that you're going to give us a dance at Mount Prospect?" she began. "Why, you're a wonderful woman for dissipation! We'd all be dying down with dulness only for you."

Mrs. Jackson-Croly, metaphorically speaking, descended with one leap from the pedestal on which she had hitherto posed for my benefit. Forgetful of the demeanour befitting one who moved in vice-regal circles, she dragged her chair, still seated upon it, across the floor, till she had placed herself knee to knee with Miss Burke, and they were soon deep in calculation as to the number of " dancing gentlemen " who could be relied on for the forthcoming ball.

A few days afterwards, Nugent O'Neill rode over to ask Willy and me to lunch at Clashmore on the following day. I had once or twice met him and Connie out hunting, and the latter and Henrietta had come over to call, after their dinner at Durrus. On these occasions my acquaintance with Connie had made rapid progress ;

she was a girl whom it was not difficult to
know and to like; but with her brother I
seemed to have come to a standstill. I
must admit to having felt rather disappointed at this, as since the night of the
dinner-party I had believed that, under
favouring circumstances, he would be a
person with whom I should find myself
on many points in sympathy. On this
occasion he certainly did not carry out
my theory. After a great deal of pro-
foundly uninteresting conversation with
Willy, in which a self-respecting wish not
to be out of it alone induced me to make
a third, they both went round to the
stables, and I watched him ride away with
a return of my old resentment towards him.

Nevertheless, I had to allow to myself
that he had not been more dull than was
suitable to the subject on which Willy had
chosen to harangue him—the question of

how and where best to lay out and level a tennis-ground in the lawn at Durrus was not one which lent itself to a display of epigram, but I could not see why they should have talked about it the whole time.

I speculated with a good deal of interest on Nugent's probable demeanour at luncheon the next day. I could not make up my mind if his unenthusiastic manner was the result of conceit or of an inborn distrust of " American young ladies." It was certainly provoking that the one Irishman I had hitherto met who seemed to have a few ideas beyond horses and farming, was either too uninterested or too distrustful to expend them upon me.

" I suppose it is the arrogant timidity of these eldest sons," I reflected, with a touch of republican scorn. " I wish I could tell him that he can talk to me without fear of ulterior designs on my part."

The day of the Clashmore repast was bright and cold. Willy had put Alaska into the dog-cart to drive me there, and we all three started in very good spirits.

"Willy," I said, as we spun along the hard road, "you have never told me anything about The O'Neill. I am rather nervous at the idea of meeting an Irish chieftain in his own lair. Ought I to kiss his hand? I am sure you ought to have driven over a couple of fat oxen and a he-goat as propitiatory offerings."

"By the hokey! I'll do nothing of the sort," said Willy. "I can tell you, he is not the sort to refuse them if I did. But I've no objection to your kissing his hand, if you like."

"How kind of you!"

"And he'll have still less. Mind you, he's a great old buck, and expects every girl who goes to Clashmore to make love to him."

"Oh, Willy!" I cried, in real alarm, "for goodness' sake don't let him come near me. I never have anything to say to old men, and yet they invariably want to talk to me."

"Then, my dear, you'd better look out. The madam will have it in her sleeve for you if he's too civil; *she* doesn't approve of his goings on."

"Well, one comfort is, I shall probably be in his black books in five minutes, as you say it is one of the seven deadly sins to call him *Mister* O'Neill. I could no more call him 'O'Neill' than I could fly; I should feel as if I were talking to a coachman."

"Oh, I dare say he'd put up with more than that from you! You're just his sort. I know he'll tell every one you are 'a monstrous fine girl.' You know, he likes them tall and dark and hand——"

"Do hold your tongue!" I interposed. "You are most offensive."

"Well, never mind," said Willy, consolingly. "Maybe he won't look at you, after all. There's that big English girl we saw in church with them last Sunday—Watson, I think Nugent said her name was—I dare say he devotes himself to her all the time. Though," he added, "I don't see why I shouldn't go in for her myself"—with a glance at me to see how his shaft had sped.

"Oh, I hope you will!" I said; "it would interest me so much."

I thought Willy looked a little crestfallen, and he said no more on the subject.

As I walked cautiously across the highly polished floor of the Clashmore hall, preceded by an eminently respectable young footman, I was amused to find that my mind was occupied in unfeigned admiration of the cleanliness of the house. This, then, was the result of six weeks' residence at Durrus. I had become so inured to untidiness, and a generally lenient system of cleansing, that the most ordinary household virtues had acquired positive instead of merely negative value.

The big, bright drawing-room seemed full of strangers, who, as I came in, all stopped talking. I caught, however, my own name, spoken in a voice unmistakable, even in the undertone in which it said, "I declare, there's Miss Sarsfield herself!" and I had the uncomfortable conviction that Miss Mimi Burke, in common with the rest of the room, had been discussing me.

I advanced with uncertain speed across the wide space of glowing carpet which separated me from Madam O'Neill, my last few steps being considerably accelerated by the sudden uprisal from under my feet of an abnormally lengthy dachshund, which had lain coiled unseen in my path.

"That detestable dog of Henrietta's!" said Madam O'Neill, as she shook hands with me; "he is always getting in the way. How do you do, Miss Sarsfield? Robert dear, this is Miss Sarsfield."

A stout, elderly gentleman, in a light suit of clothes, and with one of the reddest faces I have ever seen, stepped forward with a very polite bow and expansive smile, and shook hands with me. This was my host, but the warning I had received against encouraging his attentions had so alarmed me, that as soon as was decently possible I turned my back upon him and began to talk to Henrietta. I had been aware all the time of Willy's observation, and now, as I turned and met his malevolent eye, I felt with dismay that my face was slowly turning a good fast colour, analogous to Turkey red. Deeply conscious of this, and of the unsparing glare of light from the large plate-glass windows, I spent some singularly uncomfortable moments, until the booming of the gong interrupted Miss O'Neill's comments on the weather.

I suppose that every one has at some period of their life felt the absurdity of being led forth processionally to an entirely commonplace meal, to which one is quite capable of walking unassisted on one's own legs. I was never more keenly alive to this than on the present occasion, when, thrusting my hand with some difficulty inside The O'Neill's bulky arm, and feeling at least a head taller than he, we with all dignity led the way into the dining-room.

I looked round the luncheon-table to see how people had arranged themselves. My neighbour on the right was the Reverend

Thomas Horan, Rector of Rathbarry, a dull-looking man, with a saffron complexion, and hair and beard of inky blackness, whose speech in private life was little less unintelligible than his pulpit utterances. Opposite to me sat Nugent O'Neill and Miss Watson. She was an ordinary type of smart English girl, tall, fair, square shouldered, and well dressed, and apparently rather fond of the sound of her own high, unmodulated voice. She, evidently, had no difficulty in talking to Nugent. I caught from time to time such fragments of their discourse as, " Saw your college get a bump," " Up for commemoration week," " Ladies' eights "—by which latter phrase I wondered if he were referring to her size in gloves.

The view to my right was impeded by the portly form of Miss Mimi Burke, who was next Mr. Horan, she and that divine interchanging much lively badinage, in tones suggestive of a duet between two trombones. Beyond her I could just discern the feeble profile of a red-haired youth of nineteen or twenty, who was subsequently introduced to me as Mr. Barrett.

The O'Neill had been up to this too busy in dissecting two ducks of unusually athletic physique to speak to me; but he had from time to time—

" Looked upon me with a soldier's eye,
  That liked, but had a rougher task in hand."

And when the last limb had been distributed, he turned his crimson face and gleaming eyeglass upon me.

"And why haven't we seen you out with the hounds lately, Miss Sarsfield?" he began, in a wheezy, luscious voice, with a suspicion of brogue in it. "Nugent brought home such accounts of your doings that I went out myself in hopes of seeing you show us all the way."

I modestly disclaimed all credit for the glories of the run which had made such a sensation. "And I have only been able to go out once or twice since," I added; "the meets have been so far away, and Willy has only two horses."

"Ah! I wish you'd let me give you a mount. Your father has done as much for me many a day when I was a youngster; and I think you and I ought to be great friends"—this with a gaze of deep feeling from the unglazed eye.

"Thank you; you are very kind," I murmured discomposedly, looking towards the little madam to see if she were noting the behaviour of her lord.

But no; the pink ribbons and marabout tufts of her elaborate cap were nodding complacently towards Willy, who was talking to her with enviable ease and fluency.

Willy's skill in talking to elderly ladies amounted to inspiration. At present both Madam O'Neill and Miss Bessie Burke were hanging on his words, with every appearance of rapt interest; while I, the beloved of old men, could make no fitting rejoinder to the advances of my host. "But then," I reflected, in self-extenuation, "old women are infinitely preferable to old men."

"Ah yes!" The O'Neill went on, "how much you remind me of your father! The same wonderful dark eyes—— "

"Mine are grey," I interrupted, in as repressive a manner as possible.

The objects in question immediately underwent a close scrutiny.

"No matter—no matter; they have the same depth of expression. 'That eye's dark charm 'twere vain to tell,' eh? Isn't that what Byron says?"

Of the appropriateness of the quotation my plate alone was in a position to give an opinion, as on it my eyes were immovably fixed.

"I say, sir," said Nugent, suddenly, from across the table, "did you know that Miss Watson was a great fortune-teller? You ought to show her your hand."

Nothing loth, O'Neill laid his fat white hand on the table for Miss Watson's inspection. She at once opened the campaign in a masterly manner, by pronouncing it to be that of a "flirt," and I felt that the chieftain's entertainment need no longer be a matter of anxiety to me.

Looking at his father with a peculiar expression, in which amusement seemed to predominate, Nugent listened for a minute or two to Miss Watson's ingenious insinuations and pronouncements. Then he turned to me.

"Do you believe in chiromancy, Miss Sarsfield? It seems to me an adaptable sort of science."

CHAPTER XV.

AN AMERICAN GIRL.

" She's always been kind of off-ish and partic'lar
for a gal that's raised in the woods."

LUNCHEON was over. The elders of the
party had returned to the drawing-room,
where they were seated in a state of con-
tented satiety, discussing their servants,
their gardens, and the Church of Ireland
Sustentation Fund, according to their age
and kind.

In the billiard-room, a four-handed game
was going on. Willy and Miss Watson
were playing Connie and Mr. Barrett;
and, as billiards was not one of my accom-

plishments, I preferred, notwithstanding polite offers of instruction, to sit in a window-seat and look on.

Nugent at first undertook the office of marker; but as he tried at the same time to explain the intricacies of the game to me, complications in the scoring soon arose, accompanied by violent altercations with the players. Finally, he was expelled with ignominy, it having been proved that he had marked Miss Watson's most brilliant break to her opponents.

"I thought I should never have come alive out of that," he said, sitting down in the window beside me; "Miss Watson looked as if she was going to convince me with the butt end of her cue, and I have no ambition to have a row with Willy. I shouldn't have much of a chance."

I thought, nevertheless, that he looked well able to take care of himself, as he leaned back against the window-shutter, and began to roll a cigarette, while the sun slanted in upon his light, firm figure and well-shaped head, striking a pleasant dazzle into his blue eyes as he glanced at the players.

"Do you know Mr. Jimmy Barrett?" he asked, in cautious tones, as that youth, his freckled face pink with anxiety, sprawled across the table to play his stroke.

"No, I don't know him, but I remember seeing him out hunting."

"He's a very fine rider, but that's about all he's good for. From the appearance of things at present, he will have cut the cloth in the course of the next five minutes. If Connie is going to give lessons in billiards, she ought to keep a private table for her disciples."

Nugent had laid his tobacco-pouch on the seat beside him while he was speaking; it was covered with crimson plush, and his monogram, sumptuously worked in gold thread, adorned the flap. I thought it, on the whole, rather vulgar.

"I am thankful that I was not decoyed into playing," I said. "I must say all my sympathies are with Mr. Barrett; he did not want to play in the least, and I am sure he does not look as if he were enjoying himself."

"I deny that he was decoyed into playing," said Nugent, argumentatively, lighting his cigarette and leaning back again with an air of leisurely satisfaction; "and, anyhow, he is not a case in point. The mere fact that you are an American is about fifty points in your favour. You would probably lick all our heads off by the sheer force of instinct and power of intimidation." He took up his tobacco-pouch, and looked at it absently. "Yes,

you're a great nation. For instance, this
very fine thing is of Yankee origin, and I
don't believe the worker of it had ever
done anything of the kind before. It was
done, as the Irishman played the fiddle,
' by main strength,' and yet look at it!"

"It's very *gay*," I said, regarding it
with chilly disfavour.

Nugent looked at me meditatively, as he
put it back into his pocket. " Does that
mean professional jealousy?" he asked.
" Are you also a worker of tobacco-
pouches ?"

" I can't work any more than I can play
billiards," I said, with some enjoyment of
the admission.

" No? What a pity!" said Nugent, a
little inattentively. " Do you know, I once
taught an American girl billiards, and
after she had played for a week, she used
to beat me pretty nearly every time."

"But I think I told you before I was *not* an American girl," I said energetically. "Every one here persists in calling me American, and I am nothing of the kind; I am Irish!"

"It seems to me you are very anxious to 'go back on' your native land," he said, looking at me through his half-closed eyelids; "you won't allow yourself to be called American, and you don't even speak the language."

"That is the regular British fallacy. You all expect us to talk through our noses, and say, 'Wal, stranger.'"

"Not at all. I am awfully well up in modern American fiction, and I know all about the Boston young woman and her high-class conversation. I assure you, there is no one on earth that I should be so much afraid of."

"I am sure you took that idea from

Henry James's 'Bostonians,' but they are not all as superior and conscientious as Olive Chancellor was in that. Certainly *I* am not, and I lived for a long time in Boston."

"Really!" he said, opening his eyes; " I had no idea of that. I think," he went on, after a moment's pause, "you might have mentioned it before, and saved me from giving myself away as I did."

"You have said nothing very compromising so far," I said, stooping down to help Henrietta's dachshund in an attempt to scramble on to my lap; " but I thought it kinder to warn you while there was yet time."

He laughed rather foolishly, and slowly knocked the ash off his cigarette against the window-sash. " All the same," he said, " I think I was quite right in what I said. By the way, I got a lot of new fiddle music to-day. I wonder if you would come and have a look at it? Perhaps we could try over some?"

"I am afraid it is rather late," I said hesitatingly. "I should like to do so very much, but I think the game must be nearly over, and we ought to go home then; it gets dark so quickly."

"Well, perhaps you would allow me to bring it over to Durrus some day? My sister is very slow at reading music, and I think I remember your saying that you did not mind playing accompaniments."

I did remember saying so quite well, and also the manner in which the intimation had been received; but I magnanimously determined to let bygones be bygones, and consented with a good grace.

The game was, as I had said, coming to a conclusion. Willy was playing, and evidently playing extremely well—striding round the table with silent purposeful rapidity, while Miss Watson triumphantly proclaimed the score as his break mounted. Connie, ignoring the dejection of her unhappy little partner, was leaning back against the wall, humming a little bitter tune, with the air of having lost all interest in the proceedings.

"I think Connie looks as if she had enough of Jimmy's billiard-playing," said Nugent, with brotherly discernment; "she doesn't like being beaten a bit. There's an end of Willy's break. Now, Jimmy," he called out, "they only want three of game—42 plays 97; it's a good game to win!"

Mr. Barrett advanced to the table, looking with a sickly smile to his partner for an encouragement which he did not receive. Nugent and I left our window, and came closer to see the finish of the game. We had not long to wait. Taking prolonged aim at the red ball, Mr. Barrett dealt his own a faltering tap; it rolled slowly across the table, and, without touching either of the other balls, sank unobtrusively into a side pocket.

"Three to us. Game!" said Miss Watson. "I think we did pretty well, Mr. Sarsfield. I told you you were good at games as soon as I looked at your hand."

"Why, have you had your fortune told, Willy?" I said.

"Yes," he said shortly. "Are you quite sure you've told me everything?"—turning from me to Miss Watson.

"Oh dear, no! not more than half. I shall *think* about your hand, and tell you the rest another day," said Miss Watson, with great suavity. "Irishmen's hands are so puzzling—so contradictory, you know; but I suppose all Irish people are that, aren't they?"

"Never mind, Mr. Barrett," I heard Connie saying; "we will play them again some other time. Now, good people, won't you all come and have some tea?" she continued. "You had better not lose time, or there will be none left. Mr. Horan gets through tea and cake like a Sunday school—four cups at least, and two slices with every cup! So if you and Willie are going to have any more palmistry, Georgie, we certainly shall not wait for you."

In the drawing-room, we found Madam O'Neill, Henrietta, and Mr. Horan sitting over the tea-table; the latter with his handkerchief spread over his knees, and a general greasiness of aspect suggestive of buttered toast. The Burkes had gone, and, to my unbounded relief, The O'Neill did not appear.

" It's just as I said," whispered Connie; " there isn't an atom of toast or hot cake left. Did you see mamma just now hiding the sponge-cake behind the slop-basin to get it out of his way? I see the Burkes have gone," she went on. " If you could only have heard old Mimi singing your praises before you came to-day! She said it was ' *deloightful* to have that *sweet* young creature settled in the country,' and that, ' considering you had been brought up among the Americans, you really spoke English as well as she did.' Was not that what she said, Nugent ? "

Her brother laughed, and sat down beside me.

" You see, what I told you is quite true," he said, " though perhaps I did not put it as nicely as Miss Burke did. As an

American young lady, you are a failure in these parts."

"I am delighted to hear it," I replied. "If you had not formed a preconceived idea that I was a Yankee, I know you would have noticed my Cork brogue at once."

While we were talking, Willy came up.

"Are you nearly done your tea?" he demanded. "The trap is at the door some time."

He remained standing before me, as if he expected me to get up at once. That something had annoyed him was evident, and, feeling that delay was unadvisable, I swallowed my tea with all possible despatch, and made my adieux.

Nugent came to the hall door with us.

"Then, may I come over on Tuesday?" he said, tucking in the rug for me, while Willy silently picked up the reins, and took the whip out of the rest, "or any other day that would suit you would do for—— " The rest of the sentence was lost, as Willy, without further ceremony, drove away.

" Very well—Tuesday ! " I screamed back, as we whirled down the avenue. " My dear Willy, I don't know why you were in such a desperate hurry," I went ·on, rather crossly.

" Well, how was I to know he had anything more to say ? " retorted Willy, with equal ill-temper. " I'm sure he had plenty of time to settle everything before we left the house. I wasn't going to keep the mare standing, if he chose to go on prating there."

" I don't suppose another five seconds would have done her any mortal injury, and I think you might have risked it for the sake of civility."

He did not answer, and we drove along

in silence, Willy maintaining a demeanour of unbending severity, and affecting to be altogether occupied with his driving.

" Very well," I said to myself, " if he likes to sulk, he may ; I won't take any notice of him."

No word was spoken for at least a mile. Alaska trotted steadily on, under the leafless beeches, and along the road by the sea, till she at length slackened to walk up a hill.

" Are you cold, Theo ? " Willy did not turn his head, but I felt that the olive branch had been extended.

" Not particularly," I said, as indifferently as possible.

" I put a wrap into the trap for you "— stretching a long arm over the back of the seat, and dragging a cloak from the depths. " You must be perished in that thin coat. Here, let me put this round you."

He wrapped me in it with unnecessary care, and while he was doing so he said suddenly,

"I'm awfully sorry if I was rude to you." You know that——" His voice broke, and he stopped as suddenly as he had begun. I put up my hand to fasten the cloak for myself, and was rather startled to find it caught and fervently squeezed.

"Oh!" I said, withdrawing my hand sharply, "you were not in the *least* rude to me. I did not mind a bit. We had a very pleasant day on the whole, I think," I continued inconsequently; "and did you see how beautifully I behaved to The O'Neill?"

I fancy Willy looked a little disappointed at his apology being disposed of so quickly.

"No, I can't say I did," he answered, in

an injured way. "I had plenty to do talking to the madam."

"Yes, I saw you. I was looking at you with the deepest admiration all through lunch. And, by the way, what do you think of Miss Watson? She seems to be a wonderful billiard-player."

"I thought you were too busy talking to Nugent to notice what we were doing," said Willy, with some return of sulkiness. "It didn't look as if you found it so hard to talk to him, as you're always saying you do."

"But I assure you we *were* looking at the game, Willy. I don't understand billiards, so you can't expect me to watch every stroke."

"Well, I only know that I spoke to you one time, and you were so much taken up with talking about Boston or something, that you never even heard me."

"Then you must have said it absolutely in a whisper," I said, in heated self-defence. "Mr. O'Neill was not saying anything in the least interesting, only that he should never have thought I had been brought up in America."

"H'm!" said Willy, in a more mollified tone. "He must have meant that for a compliment. *I* know what he thinks of Yankee girls. He's told me many a queer story of one he met at Cannes last winter."

We rounded a turn in the road, and in the twilight I could see the Durrus woods spreading darkly down to the sea. It would take another ten minutes to reach home, and, though Willy was simmering down, I knew that we were still on dangerous ground.

"What did Miss Watson say of your hand?" I asked, with the view of changing the conversation. "Did she tell you that you had 'no sense of humour, and homicidal tendencies, combined with unusual conscientiousness'? That's what a man once told me."

"No," answered Willy, quite seriously; "she didn't say very much about my character. She was looking at my line of heart most of the time, I think. She told me that I would have 'two great passions' in my life, and that I was to be married soon." He stopped, and looked at me.

"How exciting!" I said hurriedly. "My man did not tell me any of those interesting sort of things."

"She said my line of fate was broken," resumed Willy, "whatever that may mean. She told me I had a very good line of intellect, but it wasn't properly developed. I dare say the last part of that's true enough," he added, with a sigh. "I never got a chance to learn anything when I was a boy. The governor sent me from one dirty little school to another for a couple or three years, and then the national schoolmaster had a go at me, and that's about all the education I ever had."

"I dare say you get on just as well without being very good at classics and those sort of things. And, you see, you passed your exam. for your captaincy in the West Cork quite easily," I said, with a rather lame attempt at consolation.

"That's quite a different thing; any fool could do that. What makes me sick is to see Nugent and chaps like him, who have been to Harrow and Oxford, and all the rest of it—and here I've been stuck all my life, without a chance to get level with them. It's when I'm talking to you that I feel what an ignorant brute I am!"

"I hate to hear you talk like that,

Willy," I said, really distressed. "*I* never thought you so—not for an instant. On the contrary, I think you know more than any one I ever met—about practical things; and if you don't look where you're going, you will drive over that old woman who is going in at the gate"—as we turned sharply off the road at the Durrus lodge—"and I believe it is that dreadful old Moll, too. I am thankful to say I have not seen her for ever so long."

CHAPTER XVI.

FERRETING.

"I do perceive here a divided duty."

IT was early in December, a showery, blustry afternoon; but I was sitting out of doors in the hay. The men had been cutting away the great rick in the haggard; they had taken a slice off it, down almost to the ground, and I had burrowed myself a comfortable bed among the soft trusses, with my back against the bristling, newly shorn wall of hay that towered above me like a gable. The dogs were standing beside me in different attitudes of intensest attention, their eyes fixed, like mine, upon a hole in the foundations of the rick, from which at this moment a pair of legs in corduroys and gaiters were protruding.

"Have you come to them yet?" I called out.

A muffled grunt was all that I could hear in answer; but after a moment or two, the body belonging to the legs was drawn out of the hole.

"I've got one of the brutes," said Willy, holding up his hand, with a ferret hanging limply from it. "I don't know how I'll get the other; those rats must be miles back in the rick. I'll have to go up for one of the young Sweenys to help me to move some of the stones under the rick."

"I think in that case I shall go home," I said. "I suppose you'll take hours over it."

"Oh no! Do wait a bit; we won't be

any time. You can have my coat if you're cold," said Willy, dropping the reclaimed ferret into its bag. "I'll be back in a jiffy."

He climbed the wall of the haggard, and took a short cut across the field to where the whitewashed walls of Sweeny's cottage showed through the red twigs of the leafless fuchsia hedge that incongruously surrounded it.

I took out my watch as soon as he had started, and saw that it was half-past three. Willy seemed to have forgotten that this Tuesday afternoon was the one on which Nugent had said he would come over. I had taken care to say something about it at breakfast, but had done it so lamely and inopportunely that I was not sure whether Willy had heard me; and a kind of awkwardness had prevented me from reminding him of it when he had asked me after luncheon to come out with him to the haggard, where a thriving colony of rats had been that morning discovered.

Willy and I were now on terms of the most absolute intimacy. His daily companionship had become second nature to me—something which I accepted as a matter of course, which gave me no trouble, and was in all ways pleasant. But, for all that, I had begun to find out that in some occult way I was a little afraid of him. He was unexpectedly and minutely observant, and, where I was concerned, appeared to be able to take in my doings with the back of his head. It was this gift, combined with his unostentatious acuteness, that made me sometimes feel foolish when I least wished it, and lately had made any mention of Nugent's name a difficulty to me.

At all events, at this particular moment I did not feel disposed to explain matters, and I settled myself again in the hay, hoping that the capture of the ferret would allow me, by the natural course of things, to get home in time without having to remind Willy of my expected visitor.

The demesne farm, as it was called, was at some distance from the house—at least ten minutes' walk down a stony lane, worn into deep ruts by the passing of the carts of hay; and now that the ruts had been turned into pools by heavy showers, it was anything but a pleasant walk. The boreen passed through the fields in which Willy had schooled Alaska; it came out into the road near the lodge, and thence led directly to the house, whose gleaming slate roof and tall chimneys I could see from where I was sitting, above the trees of the plantation. The short December day was already beginning to close in; the setting sun was level with my eyes, and was sending broad rays up the long slope that lay between the farm and the sea. Everything for the moment was transfigured; all the wet stones and straw lying about the yard shone and glistened. The pigs were splashing through pools of liquid gold; and the geese, who were gabbling in an undertone near the hayrick, looked blue on the shadow side, and silver-yellow on the side next the sun—one could believe them capable of laying nothing but golden eggs. The wind was going down with the sun, and it seemed as if we should have no more rain; but there was a dangerous-looking black cloud over Croaghkeenen. I wondered if Nugent had come. That cloud certainly meant rain; perhaps it would serve as an excuse to get home.

Willy was as good as his word about coming back quickly, and brought with him not one, but two small sons of the house of Sweeny, with shock heads of hair, as fluffy as dandelion seed, and almost as white, and big grey eyes that looked doubtfully at me from under the blackest lashes and out of the dirtiest faces I had ever seen in my life.

"Come, Timsy," said Willy to the smaller of the two, "in you go; and if you get a grip of him at all, hold on to him, no matter if he eats the nose off your face."

In no wise discouraged by this injunction, Timsy crawled into the hole, until nothing but the muddy soles of his bare feet were visible. But the ferret was evidently beyond human reach. I sat impatiently enough, looking on, and trying to summon up courage to say that I would go home, when I felt a drop or two of rain on my hand, and saw that the heavy cloud now shut Croaghkeenen altogether out of view, and that a thick shower was coming across the sea and along the slopes of Durrus. In another instant we were enveloped in a gusty whirl of rain.

"Run to the Sweenys', Theo!" cried Willy, jumping up from his knees, and abandoning his attempt to push little Sweeny deeper into the hole; "we must shelter there."

"Couldn't we get home?" I said, standing undecidedly in the downpour, and thinking with despair that my deserted visitor was possibly arriving at Durrus now.

"No; you'd be drowned getting there. Come on."

We ran up the lane as fast as was possible from the nature of it, with the mud splashing up at every step, the rain trickling down the backs of our necks, and the dogs racing along with us, getting

very much in the way by ridiculous jumps
at the bag in which Willy carried the
ferret, and evidently believing that this
unusual rushing through the mud was
only a prelude to something far more
thrilling. I picked my way after Willy
through the Sweenys' yard, along a path
which ran precariously between a manure
heap and a pool of dirty water, and saw
Mrs. Sweeny flinging open her door to
receive us.

"Oh, ye craytures! ye're dhrowned!
Come in asthore. Get out, ye divil!"—
slapping the bony flanks of a calf which
was trying to thrust itself into the house.
"Turn them hins out, Batty! Indeed, 'tis
a disgrace to ask ye into that dirty little
house, and me afther plucking a goose."

We entered the low, narrow doorway;
and the hens, seeing that they were
hemmed in, and disdaining even at this

extreme moment to yield to Batty's prac-
tised pursuit, took to their wings, and flew
past our heads through the doorway with
varying notes of consternation.

"Did anny wan iver see the like of
thim hins?" demanded Mrs. Sweeny,
dramatically, while she dragged forward a
greasy-looking kitchen chair. "I'm fairly
heart-scalded with them—the monkeys of
the world! Sit down, ochudth, sit down
why!" she went on, addressing me, her
broad red face beaming with pride and
hospitality. "Indeed, me little place isn't
fit for the likes of ye! Sure, wouldn't ye
sit down, Masther Willy, till I get ye a
dhrink of milk? Run away, Bridgie"—
this in an undertone to a grimy little girl
—"and dhrive in the cows."

She produced another chair for Willy,
the discrepancy in the length of whose
legs was corrected by a convenient dip in

the mud floor of the cottage, and Willy sat down, and at once began a diffuse and cheerful conversation with her.

The fates certainly seemed to be against me. This shower would probably last for some time, and it would be impossible to say that I wanted to go home until it was over. I looked at my watch; it was already nearly four. Nugent would very likely come early—he had said that he would be over some time before tea—and would hear that I had gone out, and had left no message or explanation of any kind for him. It was very exasperating, but, as long as this deluge of rain lasted, all I could do was to sit still and possess my soul in as much patience as possible.

The cabin had more occupants than, in its doubtful light, I had at first noticed. In the smoky shadow of the overhanging chimney-place was huddled, on a three-legged stool, a very small old man in knee-breeches and a tail-coat, who was smoking a short pipe, and still held in his hand the battered tall hat which he had taken off on our entrance. He was our hostess's father-in-law, one of the oldest tenants on the estate, and he sat, as I had often seen the old country men in the cabins sit, smoking and dozing over the fire, and looking hardly more alive to what was going on than the grey, smouldering lumps of turf on the hearth. In the dusky recess at the foot of a four-poster bed, which blocked up one of the small windows, Batty and two other children were hiding behind each other, and were staring at us as young birds might. Pat and Jinny were vulgarly snuffing among Mrs. Sweeny's pots and pans, with an affectation of starvation which but ill-assorted with what I knew of their recent luncheon. Now they had come, with stunning unexpectedness, on a cat, crouched on the dresser, and, when called off by Willy on the very eve of battle, remained for the rest of their visit in agonized contemplation of her security. From a hencoop in the corner by the bed came faint cluckings; the goose which Mrs. Sweeny had been plucking lay with its legs tied beside the red earthen pan, in which it might have seen its own breast feathers, and tried to console itself by pecking feebly at the yellow meal which had been spilt on the ground in front of the chickens' coop.

Mrs. Sweeny was sitting on a kind of rough settle, between the other window and the door of an inner room. She was a stout, comfortable-looking woman of about forty, with red hair and quick blue eyes, that roved round the cabin, and silenced with a glance the occasional whisperings that rose from the children.

"And how's the one that had the bad cough?" asked Willy, pursuing his conversation with her with his invariable ease and dexterity. "Honor her name is, isn't it?"

"See, now, how well he remembers!" replied Mrs. Sweeny. "Indeed, she's there back in the room, lyin' these three days. Faith, I think 'tis like the decline she have, Masther Willy."

"Did you get the doctor to her?" said Willy. "I'll give you a ticket if you haven't one."

"Oh, indeed, Docthor Kelly's afther givin' her a bottle, but shure I wouldn't let her put it into her mouth at all. God knows what'd be in it. Wasn't I afther throwin' a taste of it on the fire to thry what'd it do, and Phitz! says it, and up with it up the chimbley ! Faith, I'd be in dread to give it to the child. Shure, if it done that in the fire, what'd it do in her inside ? "

" Well, you're a greater fool than I thought you were," said Willy, politely.

" Maybe I am, faith," replied Mrs. Sweeny, with a loud laugh of enjoyment. " But if she's for dyin', the crayture, she'll die aisier without thim thrash of medicines ; and if she's for livin', 'tisn't thrusting to them she'll be. Shure, God is good—God is good—— "

" Divil a betther ! " interjected old Sweeny, unexpectedly.

It was the first time he had spoken, and having delivered himself of this trenchant observation, he relapsed into silence and the smackings at his pipe.

" Don't mind him at all, your honour, miss," said his daughter-in-law, seeing my ill-concealed amusement. "Shure, he's only a silly owld man."

"He's a good deal more sensible than you are," said Willy, returning to the subject of Honor.

The rain poured steadily down. I thought of Nugent, and could fancy his surprise at hearing that I was not at home. It was not, I argued to myself, so much that I was sorry to miss him, as that I hated being rude; and it certainly was rude to have gone out on the day he had settled to come, without even leaving a message. What an amazing gift of the gab Willy had! Rain or no rain, it was clear that he and Mrs. Sweeny meant to talk to one another for the rest of the afternoon.

The old man in the chimney-corner had watched me during all this time, and muttered to himself every now and then —what, I could not understand. We must have been sitting there for ten minutes at least, when the two boys whom Willy had left to look for the ferret came dripping in, with the object of their search safely housed in a bag, and silently stationed themselves along with their brothers and sisters in the corner by the bed.

"Is the rain nearly over?" I asked the elder.

"I dunno, miss," he replied, bashfully rubbing the sole of his foot up and down the shin of the other leg.

"I can tell you that," said Willy, getting up and going to the door. "I don't think it looks like clearing for another quarter of an hour."

"Then I don't know what I can do," I said, in unguarded consternation.

"Why," said Willy, turning round and looking at me with his hands in his pockets, "what's the hurry?"

"There is no hurry exactly," I said, feeling very small and cowardly; "but I thought you knew—at least, I think I told you this morning, that Mr. O'Neill said he would come over to-day."

I wondered if this simple sentence gave any indication of the effort it was to me to say it.

"I can't say I remember anything about it," Willy answered, in what I am sure he thought a crushingly chilly voice.

"Oh yes, indeed I did tell you," I said, getting up and following him to the door; "but you sneezed just as I was saying it, and the voice is not yet created that could be heard through one of your sneezes."

I knew that he was rather proud than otherwise of his noisy sneezes, and I laughed servilely, and looked up, hoping that he would laugh too. But there was nothing approaching to amusement in his face. It was red and forbidding, as he looked out into the rain that was thrashing down in the dirty yard. He had still a good deal of hay and hayseed about his coat and hat, and altogether I thought it was not one of his most becoming moments.

"I don't know if you'd like to start in that," he said; "but if you would, I'm quite ready to go with you."

If I had been alone, I should probably have faced a wetting in order to get back to the house; but now I was both too proud and too shy to accept Willy's offer.

"I think I shall wait a little longer," I said, going back to my chair by the fire.

"Himself's afther sayin'," said Mrs. Sweeny, as I sat down, "that he'd think 'twas your father he was lookin' at, an' you sittin' there a while ago."

Old Sweeny removed his pipe from his lips, and cleared his throat.

"Manny's the time I seen the young masther sit there," he said, in a sort of harsh whisper, turning his bleared and filmy old eyes towards me—"the way she"—he pointed a crooked forefinger at me—"is now, afther he bein' out shootin' or the like o' that; 'Be domned to ye, Sweeny, ye blagyard,' he'd say to me, 'dickens a shnipe is there left on yer land with your dhraining; I'll have ye run out of the place,' he'd say. That's the very way he'd talk to me, as civil and pleasant as yerself. Begob, ye have the very two eyes of him, an' the grand long nose of him!"

I acknowledged the compliment as well as I knew how, and old Sweeny went on again, punctuating his sentences with long and noisy pulls at his pipe.

"Faith, there was manny a wan of the Durrus tinants would rather 'twas their

own son was goin' to Ameriky than him
when he went; and manny a wan too
that'd have walked to Cork to go to his
funeral. That was the quare comin' home
that he had—to die an' be berrid in the
town o' Cork. I'll niver forget that time.
Shure the night he died in Cork—'twas
the night before the owld masther dyin' too
—I wasn't in me bed, but out in the shed
with a cow that was sick. There was
carridges dhriving the Durrus avenue that
night," he said, his voice getting lower and
huskier; "I heard them goin' the road, an'
it one o'clock in the morning! And the
big shnow comminced afther that agin."

"What carriages were they?" I asked,
with a little superstitious shiver.

The old man looked furtively round, and
took his pipe out of his mouth.

"God knows!" he said mysteriously;
"God knows! But they say there do be

them that wait for the Sarsfields agin
they're dyin'. There was wan that seen
the black coach and four horses goin'
wesht the road, over the bog, the time the
owld man—that's Theodore's father—died;
and wansht," he went on impressively,
" there was a Sarsfield out, that time the
Frinch landed beyond in Banthry Bay, and
the English cot him an' hung him; but
those people took him and dhragged him
through hell and through det'th, and me
mother's father heard the black coach
taking him wesht to Myross Churchyard."

Old Sweeny had let his pipe go out
during the telling of the story, and he left
me to make what I could of it, while he
poked about for a piece of burning turf
wherewith to rekindle his pipe. Willy
was still standing by the door.

" I think it's cleared up enough for you
to start now," he said coldly, " and if you

want to get back to the house, you'd better start before it comes on heavy again."

"Oh, very well, if you like," I answered, with equal indifference. "Good afternoon, Mrs. Sweeny."

Mrs. Sweeny was taking a bowl from the dresser, from which haven of refuge she had driven her cat with one swing of her brawny arm. It shot past Willy out of the door, followed by a flying white streak, which inference rather than eyesight told me was composed of the pursuing Pat and Jinny.

"Look at that, now!" remarked the cat's mistress; "that overbearin' owld cat'd be sittin' there, thwarting thim dogs, and she well able to run for thim; an' I wouldn't begridge them to ketch her nayther. She's a little wandhering divil that have no call to the place." She came forward with the bowl in her hand.

"See here, Masther Willy; here's eight beautiful pullet's eggs, the first she iver laid, an' you'll carry them wesht to the house for Miss Sarsfield to ate for her brekfish—mind that, now!" She gave him a slap on the back. "Och, there's no fear but he'll mind!" she said, winking at me. "He'd do more than that for yourself, and small blame to him!"

Willy took the bowl from her without taking any notice either of the innuendo or the slap which accompanied it, and marched out of the house with sulky dignity.

CHAPTER XVII.

POTATO CAKES.

"The tenacious depths of the quicksand, as is usual in such cases, retained their prey."

THE rain was not by any means over when we came out into the field. It was half-past four, but, though the sun had sunk, the clouds had lifted, and the misty orange light of the after-glow filled the air. A slim scrap of a moon had slipped up over the hill to the eastward, and the bats were swooping round our heads as we picked our way across the muddy yard of the demesne farm.

" I think you'll find the field drier than

the bohireen," said Willy, in the same distant voice which he had last spoken; "we can get over the wall here."

He took my hand to help me over, but dropped it as quickly as possible, and walked on with unnecessary haste, keeping a little in front of me. The field was, as he had said, rather better than the lane, but my feet sank in the soaked ground, the pace at which we were going took my breath away, and I began to be left behind. Willy still stalked on unrelentingly, with the enviable unpetticoated ease of mankind in wet weather.

"I wish you wouldn't go so fast," I called out at last. "I can't possibly keep up if you go at that pace."

He slackened at once.

"I thought you wanted to go fast," he answered, without looking back.

"I don't particularly care," I said, as I

struggled up alongside of him. "I should think Mr. O'Neill must have gone home some time ago."

Willy made no comment. I took out my handkerchief and wiped the last rain-drops from my face, feeling a good deal aggrieved by his behaviour.

"Your cap's all wet too," he said, looking down at me from under his eye-lids—"soaking, and so is your coat," putting his hand on my shoulder for a moment. "I think I ought to have carried you home in a turf-basket. Look at this bad bit here we've got to go through."

"Thank you," I said snappishly, taking off my wet cap and shaking the rain from it as I went, "I should rather not. I am about as wet as I can be now. It certainly was capital weather to go out ferreting in."

We were now at the "bad bit" of which Willy had spoken,—a broad, dark stripe, vivid green by daylight,—across a hollow in the field, with a gleam of water here and there in it.

"You'd much better let me carry you over this," said Willy, stopping.

"No, thank you," I said again, eyeing, however, with an inward tremor, the long distances between the tussocks of grass which might serve as stepping-stones. "You have the eggs to carry, and I have no wish to be dropped with them into the bog."

"Ah! nonsense now; you know there's no fear of that," he said, and put his arm round me as if to lift me. "Do let me."

"I am *not* going to be carried," I said, with determination. "If you'd only let me alone, I should get over quite well."

He did not take his arm away, and bent down over me.

" You're always getting angry with me these times," he said.

" No, indeed I'm not," I answered, trying to speak pleasantly, and to move forward at the same time.

His quick breathing was at my ear, and for one moment his lips touched my hair; the next I was floundering with a burning face through the deepest of the quagmire. At every step my feet sank ankle-deep; I dragged out each in succession with an effort that nearly pulled my boots off, and when I gained firm ground again, my feet had become shapeless brown objects, weighed down with mud, with which my skirt was also thickly coated. Willy had made no further effort to help me, and, having followed me across with caution, walked silently beside me as I hurried along, trying to ignore my uncomfortable and ignoble plight.

But one field now divided us from the road, and as I scrambled up on to the high fence I heard wheels, and saw something moving along it away from the Durrus gate.

"That must be Mr. O'Neill's trap!" I cried excitedly, jumping down after Willy, who was already in the field. "Oh, Willy, do run and stop him! I *must* explain——"

"There's no earthly use in trying to catch him now," Willy answered morosely. "I'm not going to kill myself running after him, like a fool, for nothing at all."

"Very well," I rejoined; "if you won't go, I will."

My indignation with Willy alone sustained me through that dreadful run. I had to cut diagonally across the field in order to intercept Nugent. The ground was soft and sticky; my mud-encumbered skirt clung round me; and I should have had scant chance of catching him but for the fact that the road, curving a little at this point, led over a steep and stony bit of hill. I reached the wall of the field just as the horse was breaking into a trot at the top of the hill; but, fortunately for me, the groom at the back of the dog-cart saw the walking-stick which I feebly brandished to attract his attention—I had no breath wherewith to shout—and, recognizing me, called to his master to stop.

Nugent pulled up, and, turning round, took off his hat with a face of such astonishment that I became all at once aware of the appearance which I must present, but I came forward with a gallant attempt to appear unconscious of my heated face and general dishevelledness.

"How are you?" I panted. "I intended

to be at home. Won't you——?" Here my breath failed me, and I was obliged to eke out my sentence with a gesture in the direction of Durrus.

"Oh, thanks; it doesn't matter in the least. Don't let me take you back any sooner than you had intended," replied Nugent, in a voice that told he had been nursing his wrath to keep it warm.

"I was going home," I said, more intelligibly. "I am very sorry, but we were delayed by the rain."

He got out of the dog-cart and shook hands with me across the low wall, on the farther side of which I was standing.

"There has certainly been a pretty heavy shower," he said, looking at me uncertainly, but, as I thought, with a dawning amusement.

"Hasn't there? Awful!" I said, smearing my wet hair back behind my ears, and putting on the cap which I had clutched convulsively in my hand during my run across the field. " We had to shelter in a cottage for ever so long."

" Who is we ? "

I looked round for my late companion, but he was nowhere to be seen.

" Willy was with me," I said ; " but he declared that it was no use trying to catch you, and—and I suppose he has gone home."

Nugent said nothing, but climbed on to the wall with as much dignity as his macintosh would permit, and helped me over it. I was very unfortunate, I inwardly reflected ; I first got wet through, and then one cross young man after another dragged me over these horrible wet stone walls. However, I said aloud—

" You must come back and have some tea ; it is quite early still."

He hesitated.

"Thanks, I am not sure if I shall have time; but perhaps, in any case, you had better let me drive you home."

The step of the dog-cart was a very high one, and as I put my foot on it to get up, the full beauties and proportions of my boot—a shapeless mass, resembling a brown-paper parcel—were revealed. My eyes met Nugent's, and we both laughed, he unwillingly, I with helpless realization of my appearance.

"I am not fit to get into anything better than a pigstye or a donkey-cart," I said apologetically. "I really am ashamed of myself from every point of view, moral and physical."

"But what on earth have you been doing?" he asked, as we turned and drove towards Durrus. "Have you been out snipe-shooting in the bog with Willy?"

"No," I answered cheerfully; "something much more vulgar."

"It certainly does look more as if you and he had been digging potatoes, but I did not quite like to suggest that."

Something in his manner offended me.

"That was just it," I said, not choosing to explain. "Willy is rather short of farm hands just now, and I have had my first lesson in 'sticking' potatoes."

"I should think you will find that a useful accomplishment in Boston."

"Knowledge is power," I said combatively. "Probably the next time you see me, I shall be learning to sell pigs in the fair at Moycullen."

"Very likely. I believe Americans—I beg your pardon, I mean people from America—like to do a country thoroughly when they get there. I suppose you go in for experiments as much as the others?"

"Why, certainly! I guess that's why I came over here; I'm experimentalizing all the time."

"Really!" said Nugent, without appearing to notice my elaborate Americanisms. "And is your experiment successful so far?" He looked me full in the face as he spoke.

"Yes, so far," I answered, with an unexplainable feeling that sincerity was required of me, and noting inwardly the blue impenetrability of his eyes.

He said nothing for a minute or two; then, without any apparent connection of ideas—

"Is Willy coming home to hear us play?" he asked. "Have you taught him to appreciate high-class music yet?"

"I don't think he wants any teaching," I said, with an instinctive wish to stand up for my cousin; "he has a wonderful ear, and his taste is really very good."

"Really!" in an uninterested voice.

"Yes," I said positively; "I believe he has a real talent for music, if he had only been given a chance."

"He did not get much of a chance at anything, I believe," Nugent said, in what seemed to me a patronizing way.

"No, he certainly did not. I think very few people know all the disadvantages he has had, and I am quite sure that very few people would have done as well as he has if they had been in his place." This with some warmth.

"I am sure I shouldn't, for one," replied Nugent, quietly taking to himself the generality which I had thought both telling and impalpable. "But then, I dare say——Why, there he is!" interrupting himself, as we turned into the avenue and came in sight of Willy, who was walking very fast towards home.

He got out of our way without looking back, and only nodded to us as we passed. I saw the bowl of eggs in his hand, and knew by the defiant way in which he carried it that he was ashamed of it.

"Your fellow-labourer seems to have had a peaceful time collecting eggs whilst you were sticking the potatoes," said Nugent, with again the suggestion of a sneer. "He certainly does not look as if he had done as much hard work as you."

"No; he has not run all the way across a field, as I did just now."

Nugent coloured. "I deserved that," he said, and laughed. Then, after a moment's pause, "And I don't think I did deserve your taking such trouble to stop me."

"Of course, you may have some inner sense of unworthiness," I answered, mollified, "that must remain between you and your own conscience; but it was very rude of me not to have been at home, and I did not mind the run half so much as writing the letter of apology which I should have felt you had a right to."

"And which I should not have believed," said Nugent. "It was so wet that I should have been quite certain that you were sitting over the fire with Willy all the time, and told Roche to send me away because you felt as if playing violin accompaniments would be a bore."

"Appearances would have been against me," I admitted; "but I should have enclosed my boots as circumstantial evidence"—advancing one disreputable foot from beneath the rug—"and perhaps also one of the potato-cakes which I had ordered specially for your benefit."

A loud twanging snap from the violin-case under the seat startled us both.

"By Jove!" exclaimed Nugent; "that is the E string, and I have not another with me."

"Then we can't have any music," I said, with unaffected dismay. "What a pity! So I brought you back for nothing, after all."

"Don't say nothing," he said; "think of the potato-cakes!"

"That may be your point of view," I said regretfully; "but when I was running across that field I was thinking of Corelli."

"I had hoped," remarked Nugent, looking sideways at me, as he pulled up at the hall door, "that you might have had some incidental thoughts about the way in which you had treated me."

"I cannot argue any more until I have had my tea," I said, getting out of the trap, and trying to stamp some of the mud off my boots on the steps.

"Perhaps I had better go home," he suggested. "As Corelli is out of the question, I suppose I shall not be wanted."

"Just as you like."

"But I want the potato-cake you promised me."

"Then, I think you had better come in and get it," I said, going into the house. "I don't approve of outdoor relief."

PART II.

THE COST OF IT.

CHAPTER I.

MRS. JACKSON-CROLY AT HOME.

"Fate's a fiddler, life's a dance."

"O'Rorke's noble feast will ne'er be forgot
By those who were there, and those who were not."

IT was the day of the Jackson-Crolys' dance, for which we had in due course received our invitations, gorgeously printed on gilt-edged cards. Willy and I were sitting over the library fire after tea, and had already begun to contemplate the combined horrors of dressing for a ball and eating a half-past six o'clock dinner, when Uncle Dominick stalked in, with a basket in his hand, which he handed to me with a note, saying austerely that one of the Clashmore servants had just ridden over with it.

The note was from Connie.

"MY DEAR THEO," it began—I had seen a good deal of the O'Neills lately, and Connie and I had arrived at calling each other by our Christian names—" we are sending you over some yellow chrysanthemums, as you said you were going to wear white. Mamma will, of course, be delighted to chaperon you, and thinks you had better come here first, and drive on in our carriage; and we can take you home and put you up for the night, as Willy may want to stay later than you do. Nugent is, I think, very proud of the bouquet. He constructed it himself, and has spent the greater part of the morning over it in the conservatory. Certainly, as far as wire goes, it is all that can be desired; there are at least ten yards of that in it."

"I should have thought you might have found some flowers for your cousin here, Willy," remarked Uncle Dominick, while I was reading the letter to myself.

"There's nothing fit for any one to wear," answered Willy, gloomily. "I was out this morning to see, and there was nothing but a few violets."

"I am sorry you did not pick them," I said, with pacific intention; "I should have been very glad to wear them. They think it would simplify matters if I slept at Clashmore to-night," I went on. "I think it would be a good plan, if you don't mind, Uncle Dominick?"

"It is entirely for you to decide, my dear," he said coldly; "you can make any arrangements that you like. The man is waiting for an answer."

"Well, I *will* sleep there," I said, goaded to decision by his ungracious manner.

I accordingly wrote a note to Connie to that effect, and, having sent it, went up to dress.

With the aid of the ministrations of Maggie, the red-haired housemaid, who had developed a deep attachment for me, I was arriving at the more advanced stages of my toilet, when I heard a knock at my door.

"I've got you some violets," said Willy's voice, "but I'm afraid they're not up to much. I've left them outside."

I heard him run down the passage to his own room, and, opening the door, I saw a small bunch of violets lying on the ground. I picked them up; there were very few of them, and they were drenched with rain. Willy must have been all this time toilsomely searching for them with a lantern in the dark.

"Has it been raining, Maggie?" I asked.

"'Deed, then, it has, miss, and teeming rain this half-hour."

So he must have gone out in the rain to pick them for me. Poor Willy!

I fastened them into the front of my dress with a sudden ache of pity, and looked at those other flowers on my dressing-table, the feathery golden chrysanthemums showing through a mist of maidenhair, with something that was near being distaste. Their coming had not been altogether a surprise to me; in fact, I had been more or less looking out for them all day. But somehow Willy's bunch of violets had taken away most of my pleasure in them, and when I came downstairs I laid the bouquet with my wraps, out of sight, on the hall table.

We hurried through our early dinner, but before we left the dining-room I received a mysterious intimation from Roche to the effect that Mrs. Rourke would like to see me outside.

Mrs. Rourke was the cook, and, inly marvelling what she could have to say to me, I went out into the hall. There, to my no small surprise, I was confronted, not only by Mrs. Rourke, but by the whole strength of the Durrus indoor establishment. There they all were—housemaid, dairy-maid, and kitchen-maids, with their barefooted subordinates lurking behind them, and from them, as I appeared, a low-breathed murmur of approval arose.

" Well, miss," began Mrs. Rourke, in tones of solemn conviction, " ye might thravel Ireland this night, and ye wouldn't find yer aiqual ! Of all the young ladies ever I seen, you take the sway ! "

"Glory be to God! 'tis thrue!" moaned a kitchen-maid, in awestricken assent.

"Why, you can't half see her there, Mrs. Rourke," said Willy, coming out of the dining-room; "hold on till I get a lamp."

He came back with the tall old moderator lamp from the middle of the dinner-table, and, holding it up, stood so that the light should fall full on me. Seldom have I felt more foolish than I did at that moment; but I did my best to live up to the position.

"And what I say, Masther Willy," continued Mrs. Rourke, taking up her parable in the manner of a prophetess, "is that I never seen a finer pair than the two of ye, and ye do well to be proud of her! And I hope it won't be the last time I'll see herself and yourself going out through that door together—nor coming in through it nayther!"

This dark saying was received by the

chorus with various devotional expressions of satisfaction.

"Yes, Mrs. Rourke," said my uncle's voice from behind me, in tones of unusual affability, "I think we have no reason to be ashamed of our representatives."

I was beginning to feel that I could bear this dreadful ceremonial no longer, when, with sincere inward thanksgiving, I heard the grinding of wheels on the gravel.

"There is the carriage," I said, turning to Willy, who had all this time been silently holding up the lamp; "do put down that thing, and get me my cloak."

My uncle himself put my wraps upon me, and stood with me in the open doorway while Roche laid a strip of carpet down the wet steps. As I stood waiting in the doorway, I saw a woman standing in the rain, just outside the circle of light thrown from the carriage lamps. She pressed forward a little as I came down the steps, and then drew quickly back with what sounded like a sob. The momentary gleam of the carriage lights had shown me who it was.

"Willy," I said, as we drove away, "did you see Anstey Brian standing there? I am almost sure she was crying. What could have been the matter with her?"

"You must have made a mistake," he said; "maybe it wasn't Anstey at all. Anyhow, if she wants to cry, there's no need for her to go and stand out there in the rain to do it."

He spoke with an annoyance that puzzled me. I was quite certain that I had seen Anstey; but, remembering that for some reason the subject of Moll Hourihane and her daughter had always been an unfortunate one with Willy and my uncle, I said no more.

We had been asked to the Jackson-Crolys' for nine o'clock, but, although it was not much more than half-past when the Clashmore carriage arrived at Mount Prospect, several heated couples whom we encountered in the hall were proof that the dancing had already been going on for some time. On coming down from the cloak-room, we saw at the foot of the stairs a small, bald-headed gentleman, moving in an agitated way from leg to leg, and apparently engaged in alternately putting on and taking off his gloves.

" That's Mr. Jackson-Croly," whispered Connie, rapidly; " he's an *odious* little being ! Don't dance with him if you can possibly help it. I always tell lies to escape him; I lose less self-respect in that way than by dancing with him."

She had no time to say more, as Madam O'Neill had by this time advanced upon

our host with a benignity of aspect born
of the consciousness of a singularly
becoming cap and generally successful
toilette. For a moment I thought he was
going to make her a courtesy, so low was
his reverence on shaking hands with her.

"It was *so* kind of you to come, Madam
O'Neill," he said, speaking through tightly
closed teeth in a small, deprecating voice;
"and the weather so unpleasant, too; yes,
indeed! But we've quite a nice little
number of friends dancing in there already,
and we're expecting another carful of
partners for the young ladies "—with a bow
to Connie and me—"from the bank in
Moycullen."

"That will be delightful!" said Connie,
with a brilliant smile, giving me at the
same time an expressive pinch.

She was looking very pretty, and was
in the highest spirits, consequent, as I

soon found, on an advanced flirtation with a Captain Forster, then staying at Clashmore. Pending his arrival, however, she condescended to dance with Mr. Jimmy Barrett, who, his usual red-hot appearance accentuated by the fact that he was wearing the hunt uniform, had waylaid us in the hall, and he now carried Connie off, while I followed the Madam and Mr. Jackson-Croly into the drawing-room. There we were received by Mrs. Jackson-Croly, imposingly attired in ruby silk and white lace. Unlike her obsequious spouse, Madam O'Neill's diamonds and acknowledged social standing had no over-aweing effect upon her, and in her greeting to us she abated no whit of her usual magnificence of manner.

" 'Twas too bad Miss O'Neill was from home and couldn't come," she observed condescendingly. " I have lots of gentlemen looking for partners—quite an '*embrasse de richesses.*' There were so many asking for invitations, and I didn't like refusing. You must let me present some of them to you, Miss Sarsfield."

The two rooms in which the dancing was going on were brightened by the red coats of several members of the Moycullen Hunt, and one of these was presently captured by Mrs. Croly and introduced to me. While I was putting his name down for a dance, the rest of our party were ushered in by Mr. Jackson-Croly.

"The Clashmore gentlemen, Louisa, my dear," he announced, with chastened pride.

The O'Neill soon made his way to me.

"Well, Miss Sarsfield, what are we to have? I see the next is a polka. I can't manage these new-fashioned waltzes, but I flatter myself I *can* dance a polka."

With inward trepidation I consented,

and was occupied with the usual difficulty of refastening my pencil to my card, when card and all were quietly taken out of my hand.

"Now, Theo, how about those dances you promised me? I'm just going to put my name down for them"—scribbling away on my card as he spoke.

"Nonsense, Willy; give me back my card at once."

"No fear; not till I've done with it. Well, this will do for a start," he said, at length returning me my card, black with his initials, and departing without giving me time to remonstrate. As he went away, Nugent came up.

"Can you give me a dance?" he asked. "I am afraid it is not very likely, after the amount of time Willy has spent over your card. I never saw him write so much before in his life; he looked as if he were writing a book."

"Oh, I think I have some left," I said, resolving to do as I thought fit about Willy's dances.

"Then, may I have 6, 11, 13, and 18, if you are here; and supper?"

"I am afraid I can't give you supper," I said, glancing at the large " W " scrawled through the four supper extras on my card; "but you can have the others, I think."

"Thanks; that is very good of you. I think the next thing to be done is to ask Mrs. Croly for a waltz"—making a survey of the room as he spoke. "I always do, and she always pretends to strike me with her fan, and says, 'I suppose you're mistaking me for Sissie,' and is arch. I should watch if I were you; I am sure you would like to see her looking arch."

I was, unfortunately, not privileged to see this phase of my hostess, as The O'Neill had already stationed himself beside me, so as not to lose a bar of his polka.

" Lots of people here to-night, Miss Sarsfield. You must feel as if you were back in Boston, eh ? Ah, there's the music ! Let us start while we have plenty of room."

He danced with the self-assertive vigour peculiar to small fat men, and we stamped and curvetted round the room in circles so small that I found it difficult to keep on my feet.

" That wasn't bad," he gasped complacently, as we staggered to a corner and rested there, while he mopped his purple forehead. " You dance like a fairy, Miss Sarsfield. But, upon my soul, I think they get more pace on every year. That woman at the piano — Mrs. What's-her-name ? Whelply, isn't it ? — why, she's rattling away as if the devil was after her."

Looking about me, I saw with deep amusement that Willy had selected Miss Mimi Burke as his partner, and was charging with her through the throng at reckless speed. Her face, blazing with heat and excitement, showed no unworthy fears for her own safety; and as, with her chin embedded in Willy's shoulder, they sped past, she cast an eye of exhilarated recognition at me.

"By Jove!" wheezed O'Neill, still breathless from his exertions; "old Mimi's got a wonderful kick in her gallop still. She's getting over the ground like a three-year-old!"

To me the appearance of my cousin and his partner was more suggestive of a large steamer going full speed through smaller craft, Miss Mimi's rubicund face representing the port light; but I kept this brilliant idea to myself.

"I hope Willy knows how to steer," I said. "He does not take things so easily as your son appears to do."

Nugent was performing what was only too evidently a duty dance with one of the Misses Jackson-Croly—a very young lady, with fuzzy hair and a pink frock. They wound sadly along, as much as possible on the outskirts of the darting crowd, Nugent's expression of melancholy provoking his more agile parent to a laugh of mingled contempt and self-complacency.

"Take things easily!" he repeated; "why, he's a regular muff. Who'd ever think he was a son of mine? If *I* were dancing with a spicy little girl like that, I wouldn't look as if I were at my own funeral. Shall we have another turn?" and before I had time for a counter suggestion we were again hopping and spinning round the room.

I had no reason to complain of lack of attention on the part of my hostess, and I and my card were soon in a state of equal confusion. The generic name of Mrs. Jackson-Croly's "dancing gentlemen" appeared to be either Beamish or Barrett, and had it not been for Willy's elucidation of its mysteries, I should have thrown my card away in despair.

"No, not *him*. That's *Long* Tom Beamish! It's *English* Tommy you're to dance with next. They call him English Tommy because, when his militia regiment was ordered to Aldershot, he said he was 'the first of his ancestors that was ever sent on foreign service.'"

Willy's dances with me were, during this earlier part of the evening, sandwiched with great regularity between those of the clans Beamish and Barrett, and I found him to be in every way a most satisfactory partner. He was in a state of radiant amiability, and proved himself of inestimable value as a chronicler of interesting facts about the company in general. He was, besides, strong and sure-footed— qualities, as I had reason to know, not to be despised in an assemblage such as this. I carried for several days the bruises which I received during my waltz with English Tommy. It consisted chiefly of a series of short rushes, of so shattering a nature that I at last ventured to suggest a less aggressive mode of progression.

"Well," said English Tommy, confidentially, "ye see, I'm trying to bump Katie! That's Katie"—pointing to a fat girl in blue. "She's my cousin, and we're for ever fighting."

There seemed at the time nothing very incongruous about this explanation. There was a hilarious informality about the whole entertainment that made it unlike any I had ever been at before. Every one talked and laughed at the full pitch of their lungs.

An atmosphere of utmost intimacy pervaded the assemblage, and Christian names and strange nicknames were bandied freely about among the groups in the corners. The music was supplied by volunteers from the ranks of the chaperons, at the end of each dance the musician receiving a round of applause, varying in volume according to the energy and power of endurance displayed. The varieties of style and time thus attained were almost unimaginable, and were only equalled by the corresponding vagaries of the dancers, whose trampings and shufflings and runnings were to me as amazing as they were unexpected.

I could see Madam O'Neill sitting in state at the end of the room, surrounded by lesser matrons, her boredom only alleviated by the acute disfavour with which she viewed the revels.

"Do you know where Connie is, my dear?" she said, with pale asperity, as I came up to her after a dance. "I have not seen her for the last four dances."

I was well aware that Connie and Captain Forster had long since established themselves in the conservatory, but Madam O'Neill was too full of her grievance to give me time to reply.

"I am perfectly horrified at what you must think of all this," she went on. "Even here I never saw such a noisy, romping set. You know, we are quite in the backwoods here—all the *nice* people live at the other end of the county—and you mustn't take these as specimens of Irish society."

I was spared the necessity of replying by the appearance of Nugent.

"Nugent, *where* is Connie?" demanded the Madam again. "It is too bad of her to make herself so remarkable in a place like this."

"Oh, she's all right; she's with Forster somewhere," he answered, with the incaution of total indifference. "Here's your host coming to take you in to supper, and I advise you to avoid the sherry. This is our dance, No. 11," he said to me. "We had better not lose any more of it."

END OF VOL. I.

PRINTED BY WILLIAM CLOWES AND SONS, LIMITED,
LONDON AND BECCLES.   G., C. & Co.

www.ingramcontent.com/pod-product-compliance
Lightning Source LLC
Chambersburg PA
CBHW031040120726
47905CB00007B/2253